The Circling Song
A Novella
By
Russell Cruse

First Printing: 2011

ISBN 978-1-4709-0996-3

He sings the sap, the quicken'd veins;
The wedding song of sun and rains
He is, the dance of children, thanks
Of sowers, shout of primrose-banks,

And eye of violets while they breathe;
All these the circling song will wreathe,

And you shall hear the herb and tree,
The better heart of men shall see,
Shall feel celestially, as long
As you crave nothing save the song.

George Meredith: The Lark Ascending

Prologue Winter 1914

Wednesday December 19th 1914

Sir Maxwell has told me that I should keep a journal. He says it may help. I don't think that it will. Although he is an approachable gentleman and not so stuffy as one might think, he is a doctor and although I'm sure he wants to help me, I believe that his true motive is to try to understand what is wrong with me. Wrong? When I regained consciousness, I could have cried with joy! To be alive and to be whole and to be unafraid! Only later did I realise that I might not be the same man I had been scant hours before; that he was gone forever. And that soon I would not care.

Although it is not visible, I can clearly remember everything from before; home, parents, friends, comrades. The thoughts make pictures in my mind, yet before of course, there was no "seeing" as I see now. There was no "knowing" as I know now. But there is remembering. Remembering how the patrol was caught in the open; how Armitage lay dying and how he wept for his mother. Remembering Streeter giving him water, his own and his friend's hands entwined, clutching the flask between them. And Armitage, blinded by steel and blood and filth, drinking; talking between grateful gulps, to his best friend who was watching him die. Watching, until shrapnel took his head. Armitage, oblivious, carried on drinking and talking; tended by a headless corpse, until he drank and spoke no more.

There was the grief, the terror and the despair. Lawrence running, he knew not where. Back to our lines; towards the enemy; it didn't matter. He just needed to be away from that place. Staggering, falling, crawling, weeping.

He was a coward. And a hypocrite. Back on the firing step, he sighted along his rifle, seeking out a life to end. Does he truly remember the bullet? The image he has must have been drawn from his imagination, surely. But he remembers being hit and thinking he would die. Not afraid, relieved. Relieved that the nightmare was ended.

He lay in the bottom of the trench, his face in the rotting leaves, the scent of life and death mingling in his nostrils; his eyes, assailed by all the colours of the world. Gold; brown, orange; yes, even green. And red. So much red. And the leaves began to speak to him and, in a language he knew but could not understand, they began to sing to him.

He remembers waking. He could have cried with joy. He told me these things before… before he forgot them. Now Lawrence diminishes as if at a distance and I take his place.

I take my place.

I can still see the song but I feel the ability to express myself – to tell what is - slipping from my grasp. The language will not do, will not suffice. I do not wish to maintain this journal. I can write no more.

Autumn 1914

ITEM: 19/10/14 Officer's Report (excerpt), Captain John Glendenning.

Details of Action October 18th – 19th 1914

The Germans launched their raid at 23:00. The first casualties were three of our sentries, the fourth managed to raise the alarm. Fortunately, the Company had only recently been stood-down following an exercise and so the element of surprise on the enemy's part was in many ways mitigated. Arms were at the ready and the majority of the attackers were halted in the saps. A small party of Germans managed to enter the front line trench but were rapidly repulsed although not before inflicting a number of casualties on the North Derbys.

A short time after the fighting in the trench itself subsided, the Germans launched a mortar barrage. I have never before encountered this tactic. Fortunately, the majority of the men were able to find cover and (the barrage, in my view, being poorly aimed), only eight men received wounds, with one officer and two men killed in this assault.

After several minutes of return fire, the barrage ceased.

Our own patrol, which had been caught out in no-man's-land during the skirmish, returned some hours later having lost two of its number. One of the returning men immediately volunteered for sentry duty. Being a reliable man and a fine shot, I had no hesitation in accepting his offer.

As dawn was breaking, he received a wound to the head, bringing our total of casualties that night to nine dead and seventeen wounded (six seriously), whilst the enemy suffered thirteen dead and two captured.

ITEM: 21/10/14 Casualty Form

Casualty Form - Active Service
Report of Senior Medical Officer
Regiment or Corps: 38ᵗʰ Div 3/16 N.Derbys. Fusil.
Regimental No: 63759_   **Rank:**   Pte_   **Service**
from: 12/04/1914 Date: 21/10/1914
Nature of Wound: Rifle bullet to the head__
Field of Battle: Ypres, Belgium__

Details: Projectile entered the skull at a point
between forehead and right temple. It is believed
that the effect of the impact was mediated by the
fact that it appears to have ricocheted off a
makeshift armoured steel loop-hole plate, through
which our man was peering. Note should also be made
of the great distance it had travelled but the
prime factor in the man's survival must be named as
nothing so much as extraordinary good fortune. The
bullet penetrated only a small distance. It showed
no evidence of having tumbled nor had it fragmented
and deformed but intact, it became lodged in what
appears to be a small rift or natural flaw in the
temporal fissure of the cranium. This has meant
that only a small amount of bone fragmentation has
occurred, although there was evidence of a
substantial depressed fracture. The bullet was
removed without difficulty. The wound bled freely
and there is no evidence of serious infection.

The patient remained semi-conscious from the time of wounding until anaesthetic was administered and, upon awakening, appeared to be suffering no ill effects other than extensive bruising, swelling and a severe headache of which, in the circumstances, he was entitled to complain.

Recommendations: __Repatriation and observation in The Royal Middlesex Hospital, London and thence to the Military Hospital at Netley. All being well, rest and recuperation for two months. Review thereafter.

The senior M.O. believes that details of this injury should be sent to the War Ministry with the purpose of providing evidence to the committee investigating the possibility of providing troops with protective headgear.

Attachments:

1) Photograph: Patient before surgery
2) Photographs:(x3) Patient undergoing surgery
4) Diagrams: (x4) Path of projectile and damage caused to patient thereby.

Signed: __(on behalf of)__ Col Leonard Godwin M.D. F.R.C.S.___ Royal Army Medical Corps

11

ITEM: 23/11/14 Letter. George Griffin to Pte. Lawrence

George Griffin
Griffin & Cator Accountants
Sheffield,
Yorks.
23/11/1914

Pte Henry Lawrence
Block D
Royal Military Hospital
Netley
Hants

Well, Harry, your doctor tells me that you are on the mend at last! This is certainly good news for us here, especially as we had braced ourselves for yet another piece of bad news. As you will no doubt have heard, Mr. Prior and Mr. Lloyd-Jones who became casualties in the Battle of Ypres at the time you received your injury, have since succumbed and are now no longer with us. Along with Mr. Endersleigh, Mr. Baraclough and Mr. Jennings, that brings to five the number of young men of this firm who have given their lives for the cause. I need not express how proud we all are of their sacrifice.

And whilst we grieve for those men and for their families, we pause to give thanks to Providence for your own wonderful deliverance. I must tell you that when we learned of the seriousness of your wounds, Mr. Phillips, the engraver, was given your name to add to our Roll of Honour.

With what joy we learned of your escape you may scarcely imagine. It was Corporal Chalmers (Mr. Chalmers as was) who delivered the happy news. You may recall his visit to your bedside. He told us that you were remarkably cheerful, given the wound you had received. Indeed, we were delighted to be informed that you seemed to him to be thoroughly invigorated and eager to return to the fray. This is no more than we expected, Harry.

Your story has had an inspirational effect. Three of our younger employees sought to enlist the other day. They were returned by the recruiting sergeant with a flea in their ear, as the eldest is only fifteen. They had hoped to pass for nineteen; one of them even placing a wad of folded paper in each shoe in order to appear taller. They are afraid it will all be over before they get their chance but even as I chastised them for their foolishness, my heart swelled with pride, as it does for you, my dear Harry.

I do hope that when sufficient time has passed and your recovery assured, you will visit us to tell of your exploits. I shall end by assuring you that everyone at the firm wishes you well.

Yours faithfully,

Mr. George Griffin.

Winter 1914 -1915

ITEM: 05/12/14   Memorandum. Dr. John Garland to Sir Maxwell Cavendish

Sir Maxwell,

You wished to be informed of any curious incidents concerning Pte. Lawrence.

At around midnight last evening, there arrived a transport from France bearing the latest batch of wounded and as I was busying myself organising the nurses to receive the men, I turned and saw Lawrence standing at the door of Ward 7 He turned and saw me and said, "Why can I not see them, Doctor?" I answered that they were too ill to receive visitors. It was only when his smile returned that I even noted that it had been absent. He seemed to come to himself once more and asked if he might be of assistance, an offer that I gratefully accepted. At around 02:00 when the men had been settled, I invited him to take tea in the Doctors' Lounge. He is, as you know, an amiable companion, if a little peculiar in his speech and we fell talking. He asked me who the men were in Ward 7. I told him that this is where we put the unfortunate souls whose end, we believe may be imminent. He said, "It is strange that they are not visible to me." "Could you not see them?" I asked him. "No," he replied, "I'm afraid I could not." It then occurred to me that he may have been experiencing loss of vision. A cursory examination was all that was needed to determine that his vision seemed fine. I asked if he had suffered any previous visual disturbances and he told me he had not.

He asked me if any of the men placed in Ward 7 had ever recovered and I told him that, thankfully, even doctors are sometimes wrong and that I had known several men who had, with the help of God, fought their way back from the brink. "Perhaps He has a purpose for them," said Lawrence. I asked him what he meant and his speech became rambling and difficult to recount but were I to characterise it,

15

I should say that, unsurprisingly, it was spiritual, almost metaphysical in nature. However, in terms of actual conveyance of meaning, I am afraid that I could make neither head nor tail of what he had to say.

ITEM: 13/12/14 Letter. Sir Maxwell Cavendish to Major Dr. James
Pennyworth

Professor Sir Maxwell Cavendish
Royal Middlesex Hospital
London W12
13/12/1914

Maj. Dr. James Pennyworth
Royal Victoria Hospital,
Netley
Hants.

Dear James,

My dear boy, forgive me; I have left it far too
long since my last letter although, in my defence,
I would offer that we are daily receiving more and
more ghastly examples of what the Army is pleased
to call, "extreme cases" and although you may,
during your own career in the R.A.M.C. have come
across a certain number, I, mercifully, have not.
I marvel that the human body can tolerate such
monstrous usage and cannot fathom any purpose the
Almighty may have in allowing it. Although our
understanding of what horrors may be wrought by
high explosives and rifle bullets is improving by
bounds, I cannot think that the sufferings of these
young men are demanded by a loving God merely to
further our knowledge. However, to business.

I have recently taken charge of a case in which I
believe you may able to offer some assistance and
it would oblige me greatly if you would consent to
do so. I well remember your interest in the
physiology of the brain and its role in mental
conditions and I remember too, some of our more
lively discussions on the matter. You will agree,
I am sure, that you were an exasperating student at
times but one whose opinions I now concede should
be taken account of.

Obviously, at the present time, you will not be in
touch with your German colleagues. I recollect,
however, that they had a great many things to say

17

on the treatment of defectives (or the "mentally ill" as I know you prefer) and I was rather hoping that you could recommend papers that may have been written by them, (or others) on the topic of savantism.

I must stress that in no way would the subject of my concern be termed an idiot per se (although I confess he is possessed of a somewhat refreshing simplicity.) Nevertheless, he is otherwise of normal, indeed to some degree, high intellect, displaying only a slight falling off of the ability to write coherently. I would imagine it is some residual effect of the injury upon the nerves and other tissue of the eye.

Forgive my impertinence if I ask you to give the matter somewhat urgent attention. I should not like the fellow to be sent back to the front before my study is complete.

My best wishes to you for a Happy Christmas

Prof. Cavendish

Maj. James Pennyworth

Royal Victoria Hospital,

Netley

Hants.

20th December 1914

Professor Sir Maxwell Cavendish,

Royal Middlesex Hospital

London W12

Dear Professor Cavendish,

I cannot tell you how much receiving your letter pleased me; and in so many respects, although I am saddened to hear of the increase in wounded being repatriated. More so, when one considers the attrition rate from infection and straightforward neglect before they even regain the shore. Being in the business of rehabilitation, most of the fellows we have at Netley are not likely to be headed off again, although some <u>are</u>, particularly my own patients, whom I make just well enough to be declared fit and sent off to fight once more. I am certain that, before your own experiences, you would have accused me of pessimism or even lack of patriotic fervour – but, then again, perhaps not. Your bark was always so much worse than your bite, as I recall!

Forgive me, my dear old tutor; I ramble. Your request, as you see, has been dealt with as you wished, speed outracing comprehensiveness, yet as good a catalogue of work as I have to hand. You have Cajal, Golgi and our own Sherrington on the subject as well as Kraepelin, the German about whom you were once so scathing. I blush that you could offer such a feeble pun on his name, to describe what you thought of his work!

Your desire for these papers is as intriguing as it was unexpected. I wonder if you are coming to a belief that Neurology is likely to offer answers to a number of the problems that medics and commanders alike are encountering as a result of the War.

I cannot write more, my dear Professor, as I am called away. I pray you, so much as confidentiality allows, do keep me informed as to the progress of your patient and bear your old student in mind should it come to the writing of a paper!

If this reaches you in time, may I wish you a very Happy Christmas, otherwise, of course, my very best to you and to Lady Frances. That dear lady's teas live with me still.

I remain proud to call myself

Your colleague and friend

James.

ITEM: 28/12/14   Letter.   Sir Maxwell Cavendish to Major Dr. James Pennyworth

```
                        Professor Sir Maxwell Cavendish
                           Royal Middlesex Hospital
                                  London W12
```

```
28/12/1914
Maj. James Pennyworth
Royal Victoria Hospital,
Netley
Hants.
```

My dear James,

I am obliged to you for your generous response to my request of December 13th. Your package arrived on Christmas Eve and, as we were entertaining and Lady Frances had forbidden all talk of work and of the war for the duration, I had no choice but to leave it on my study table for three days before being allowed to open it. You will understand the fortitude this required as much as Lady Frances seems not to!

The selection you made appears apposite but I remain troubled as to how many of those distinguished gentlemen seem to equate being a savant with being feeble-minded. With a notable exception, most of the evidence would appear to point to a link between congenital idiocy and a facility to manipulate numbers with ease. However, the case of Gerhardt, the patient of Dr. Linz, describes a circumstance not unlike that of my own Henry Lawrence; that is, an intelligent fellow who suffered a severe physical shock to the brain but who, whilst losing some faculties, found others rather improved. In Gerhardt's case, a mining accident left him entirely paralysed in one side of his body, yet able to demonstrate unusual arithmetical skill, which theretofore he had never exhibited.

Private Lawrence has no lasting physical injury, save a small indentation in the right temple, the result of depressed fracture and scarring from the surgery around the entry wound. I have fancied that I have seen him not exactly limping, rather walking with a curious skipping gait on occasions. His commanding officer has informed me that Lawrence is a serious fellow with a head for figures, willing and consistent but showing few leadership qualities beyond an ability to organize and little in the way of physical strength. According to my informant, Lawrence looked to be in severe danger of sitting the whole thing out behind a desk in Paris. In other words, an unremarkable soldier.

Yet I feel him now to be worthy of study and would be indebted to you once more, if you would consent to collaborate with me in the matter of his treatment, such as it might be. He has expressed a desire to return to his unit and, for the while, I have been able to refuse the request on medical grounds. He is undernourished, still and has a number of minor ailments that can keep him under my care for a few more weeks. Beyond this, I may have to call in a few favours. Once I have exhausted all avenues, I shall push to have him transferred into your care at Netley as a nervous case. I will be interested to hear what you have to say about him.

Thank you, once again, for the assistance you have afforded me in this matter. I trust that your intellect (if not your purse) will be rewarded once you meet our patient.

Yours ever,

Cavendish

ITEM: 07/02/15 Letter. Sir Maxwell Cavendish to Major Dr. James Pennyworth

Professor Sir Maxwell Cavendish
Royal Middlesex Hospital
London W12

07/02/1915
Maj. James Pennyworth
Royal Victoria Hospital,
Netley
Hants.

My dear James,

As I have been foretelling in my earlier correspondence, the time has come when the Army would prefer Private Lawrence to be, once more, under its care rather than mine. I have made a request to have him sent to Netley for observation before discharging him as fit for duty. It will not give you as much time as I would have wished. I am afraid I have been rather selfish in not releasing him to you sooner. I have written to General Rawlinson — fortuitously an Old Harrovian — suggesting that information on Lawrence be sent and held by the senior medical officers (whom he will no doubt encounter in France) and that they, in turn keep us informed as to his progress. I have (with disgraceful hyperbole), intimated to the General that Lawrence's case needs to be studied in detail, that we might help to improve the design and quality of our infantry's headgear!

The annoying thing of it is that I have experienced something of a breakthrough very recently, just as the fellow is to be wrenched from my grasp. As you know, Lawrence has been keeping very much to himself. I know that he finds conversation something of a strain and he is prone to enforcing longeurs, which I tend to interrupt before he does, no matter how "long" I allow them. This evening saw the most substantial interview I have had with him to date.

24

It followed an incident, which I had witnessed earlier in the day and which I had found most singular. Briefly, the matter was this:

A nurse, attending to the men, let it be known (unwisely in my view) that this was her birthday but was unwilling to reveal her age, in spite of their not unexpected interest. She said to them, "All I shall tell is the day of my birth, that being a Monday". Immediately, Lawrence said, "So, you are twenty-four." The woman blushed to her toes and scurried off. You may think it was an ungentlemanly thing for Lawrence to have done but, for my own part, I believe the silly thing reaped what she had sown and that Lawrence had no inkling that he was doing anything other than making the most natural remark in the world.

No doubt you will have heard of this kind of feat being performed at fairs and on promenades up and down the land by such as are often mentioned in the literature you sent, that is: idiots and feeble-minded souls who, with no wit, perform not unlike animals in a circus, with neither understanding nor self-awareness. However, as I intimated in my last letter, Pte Lawrence is not one of these.

I had asked him to come to my office (significantly, our previous interviews had always taken place in a room set aside for the consultation), hoping to observe and make brief notes. However, it was not long before I realised that I should have to ask my assistant, Dr. Garland to join us in order to take comprehensive notes, making the interview a much more formal affair. It may be difficult for you to understand but there is something about Lawrence, which makes one want to be certain that one has heard him correctly. He uses language in such a precise and particular manner that one is careful not to misrepresent what he says. His are not the ramblings of a madman, of this I am convinced, yet much of what he says can seem somewhat incomprehensible at times.

The following is Garland's transcript of a part of our interview, which, where necessary, I have annotated in order to clarify matters. The only other thing you should know is that, as agitated as he might seem from his words, he was not so and indeed, for much of the time, he wore a smile. Please also remember that I know little of your "psychiatry" so do not, I pray, judge the quality of my questions!

Sir Maxwell: I couldn't fail to notice how quickly you were able to ascertain the age of the nurse who was attending you this morning. Can you explain how you were able to do so?

Pte. Lawrence: I cannot tell.

Sir M.: You have long possessed a gift for computation, have you not?

Pte. L: I have, sir. That is why my father apprenticed me to the firm of Griffin and Cator and, I presume, why they appear to think so highly of me. It surely cannot be for any other reason. (Here, he gave a cheery laugh).

Sir M.: But what I witnessed this morning was a remarkable feat of calculation. Wouldn't you agree?

Pte. L: With respect, sir, it is not "calculation" as you would understand it. Once I knew the day of her birth, it was as obvious as saying (here he indicated my desk) that this desk is brown. I simply knew it. More and more things are revealed and in subtly different ways, now. I do not know why.

Sir M.: Surely, it was a matter of extrapolation and judgment? Each year the date moves forward one day. Today is Tuesday and you worked out that her age could be neither eight, nor fourteen and that

26

she appeared to be older than eighteen but younger than thirty. But you worked it out very quickly indeed, taking account of leap-years and so-on.

Pte. L: No sir, I do not believe so.

Sir M.: Oh?

Pte. L: It could simply have been no other way. Twenty-four years have passed since the Monday on which she was born. Her age was visible to me.

Sir M.: I have heard you use that word, "visible" on several occasions. Are you yet able to explain the context in which you do so? (Lawrence offered no response to this.) And you have said that you believe it was receiving the wound that marked the commencement of this facility.

Pte. L: Sir, I can only tell you that before I was wounded, I was a reasonably expert computer; after, I am aware of mathematical certainties in a manner that I am unable to explain to anyone. It is a circumstance which I do not understand and one which, (long pause) if I am honest, (long pause) I wished for a long time to be rid of.

Sir M.: Why so? It would appear that you possess a somewhat enviable ability. My word, it took me a good twenty minutes and a sturdy pencil to replicate your feat regarding the age of that nurse! Certainly, it would help you in your chosen career, would it not?

Pte. L: Again, sir, I find it difficult to explain to you why it would not. Now, as before, if I am given figures to compute, I undertake the task in exactly the same way as I have always done using addition, subtraction, division and multiplication.

Sir M.: Which now, as I understand it, you are able to do with greater speed and accuracy.

Pte. L: No, sir.

27

Sir M.: Can you explain?   (Here, Lawrence paused again before, finally, shaking his head).

Pte. L: Sir, it is impossible.   They carry and order all that is but they do not render it visible.

Sir M.: I do not understand.

Pte. L: Nor do I, sir.

Sir M.: Then how am I to help you?   (long pause)

Pte. L: I don't believe you can help me, sir.

Sir M.: Indeed?   Do you believe I have been wasting my time these past weeks?

Pte. L: I do not.   You have an interest in me and I do not question your motives.   You are a master of your art, yet you desire to learn still more.   This is admirable.   (Here he rose from his seat and pointed out of the window.)   That boiler-house chimney over there is twenty-two feet and seven inches from the base to the tip.   It is also a truncated conical tube, of course, with a circumference of eight feet at the foot, falling away to five feet three inches at the top.   I could produce for you an accurate graph of the decline in proportion to the height of the structure.

You, yourself are five-feet seven and three quarter inches tall.   When you wear your brown boots, your height increases by half an inch.   The volume of air in this room is three-thousand, five hundred and twenty-eight cubic feet.   Since I entered this room, my pulse has varied between seventy-nine beats per minute – its current rate - and sixty-eight beats per minute.   My heart has beaten one thousand, eight hundred and seventy-two times and I have drawn eight hundred and twenty-four breaths. You, sir, have blinked six-hundred and fourteen times.   Every time you do so, sir, the world, for

28

me, changes.   It becomes a different place from
what it was one blink before.   (Remember, James,
all of this was said in a light tone of voice,
accompanied by a pleasant smile.)

Sir M.: How do I know that any of those things is
true?

Pte. L: You do not, sir.   But I do; and that is the
point.   When may I rejoin my unit, sir?

Spring 1915

Friday March 19th 1915

I have had my first meeting with Private Lawrence, Prof. Cavendish's former patient, in whom he has noticed a number of unusual traits following a serious wound, acquired several months ago.

My first impression was of a quiet, unassuming and uncomplaining soldier, who initially failed to impress me beyond the fact of his survival and recovery from such a severe injury.

He answered my questions courteously, taking several moments to gather his thoughts before doing so each time and submitted himself readily to a preliminary physical examination.

The only symptom of note appeared to be an irregular, yet frequent tendency to smile broadly and to turn his head quite sharply to the right at the same time. This, though a little odd, seems nothing more than a result of injury to nerves in the neck and face and worthy of no further investigation. It is curious that Prof. Cavendish did not mention this in any of his letters. However, I have not yet had time to peruse his medical notes, so I cannot yet say whether or not this is a new development.

Cavendish had advised that I should proceed slowly and should not appear to Lawrence to be in any way arch or devious. I have to say that by the conclusion of the consultation I was wondering what on earth had intrigued the Old Boy so! My madmen at the Middlesex had far more to offer with their apoplexies, brainstorms and fancies than this wounded soldier seems likely to present.

It was not until I had dismissed him that he said an odd thing.

He said, "Thank you, sir. You have a very pleasant speaking voice." At first, I took this as impertinence. I now wonder if it may not also have been   symptomatic.

ITEM: 22/03/15 Letter. Major Dr. James Pennyworth to Sir Maxwell
Cavendish

Maj. James Pennyworth

Royal Victoria Hospital,

Netley

Hants.

22nd March 1915

Professor Sir Maxwell Cavendish,

Royal Middlesex Hospital

London W12

Dear Professor Cavendish,

Lawrence was brought in on Friday and, although it
was already late, I saw him at once. I could say
differently and you would never know but our
association forbids me from misleading you and so I
tell you, honestly, my first impression was one of
disappointment. He is much as you described and he
may have been unsure of me but I found him a most
unprepossessing character. It was not very long,
however, before he said something regarding my
voice, which I mused upon on and off for the
remainder of the day. It seemed a non-sequitur but
the study of the mind teaches one that nothing that
is said by the patient is inconsequential.

He left my consulting room and, a moment later, I
caught sight of him on the lawn, heading towards

the imposing and ancient hornbeam that grows several yards from my window. He stopped beneath it, gazing upwards for so long that I was able to study his demeanour somewhat at my leisure. Hands in trouser pockets, jacket buttoned against the cold and fixing his scarf in place, he was gazing fixedly at a point, which appeared to be near the top of the tree; that smile of his, never disappearing and occasionally blossoming into a wide grin. Once or twice, his mouth dropped open and he rocked back upon his heels, yet never removed his eyes from the hornbeam. I returned to my papers and some minutes afterwards, in need of a book, I happened to walk by the window and glancing out, saw Lawrence in the same attitude as I had left him. My curiosity got the better of me and I stepped into the garden.

"Good evening," I ventured, as I placed myself alongside him, following his gaze.
"Doctor," said he, "what is the name of that bird?"
I could see nothing although, once he had drawn my attention to it, I could clearly hear the thrill of a song-thrush. I told him the name of the bird and he said,
"He is a wonder."
"How so?" I asked him.
"Why, listen; each phrase he sings is repeated perfectly – just once – and then discarded in

34

favour of another; entirely different and, if anything, more beautiful than its predecessor. I have been standing here for fourteen and a half minutes and I have not heard the same pattern twice. How can he have such a repertoire?"

"I am no naturalist," I told him. "I recognize him only because of a verse my mother spoke to me on many occasions. It is from Browning:

> "That's the wise thrush;
> he sings each song twice over,
> Lest you should think he never could recapture
> The first fine careless rapture!"

Lawrence smiled his broad smile. "Careless rapture," he said. "Oh no, doctor, there is nothing careless about it. He makes it visible like no other bird. More so even than the lark, until now the apotheosis of the visible." Lawrence pointed (presumably at the thrush, for I still had not managed to locate him) and said, "But he; He charms the atoms of the air. They flex and burn at the very touch of his voice."

Was this, I wonder, typical of the sort of conversation you, yourself have been having with him? I am left pondering upon whether his words are mere fancies, conjured almost at random and yet, there appears, as I believe you have already pointed out, method in his madness. One is

35

convinced that he understands the words he says whereas one is unable to share that understanding, meaning remaining just out of reach.

Do you remember telling me of his dislike of the written word? Yet a more poetic patient I cannot recall.

It would be valuable to learn a little of his personality and his interests before he received his wound, indeed, before he joined the army and, to this end, I have decided to write to his family. I shall of course, keep you informed. For the time being, Dear Professor, I shall say goodnight.

Yours ever,

James.

ITEM: 09/04/15 Memorandum. Dr John Rowbotham to Dr. James Pennyworth.

Re: Patient Pte. Lawrence.

He continues to keep his journal but only, I believe, because he respects your rank. He says that he does not like keeping it. However, he showed it to me without hesitation saying that he feared it was nonsense (as, indeed, much of it is). Both his handwriting and his grammar and spelling have deteriorated quite markedly over recent days, although he remains articulate in speech, if a little obscure at times. In discussing his journal, he speaks of "meagre marks" and "scribblings" and describes having to force his hand to answer his brain and his brain to answer the world. I confess I do not know what to make of it but, whilst I am sure he would not offer the information voluntarily, I get the impression that the loss of facility with pen and paper distresses him more than he would like us to believe.

I am sure you have noted that in the journal, he often speaks of himself in the third person and, even though I am listening carefully to what he says, I have never heard him do so in speech.

The second curious matter concerns another display of his remarkable memory. I shall recount the incident fully, as it demonstrates a number of things with regard to the nature of Lawrence and of his effect on the rest of the men, most of whom do not know quite know what to make of him.

Yesterday, the men were enjoying a game of cards. Apparently, their number was short and they asked Lawrence to sit in. Nurse Yelland said that he demurred but eventually he was persuaded to participate. It was when the game had been under way for some time, that the nurse called me to attend. I could hear raised voices as I approached,

37

in particular, that of Sergeant Charlesworth, whom you may recall. He is a rather rough fellow.

He was accusing Lawrence of cheating. Lawrence himself appeared unconcerned and was trying (one assumes) to appease Charlesworth. However, he only made matters worse. To begin with, he was wearing his smile – which, as you might imagine, was not appreciated by Charlesworth. Then, he said that it was not simply that he knew <u>Charlesworth's</u> hand but all the other hands as well. The other men in the game leaned forwards at this point but I was pleased to note smiles forming on their lips.

Then, completely innocently in my view, Lawrence proceeded to demonstrate the fact, as if it would explain everything! Another in the game, Corporal Kelly, far from being annoyed, seemed very amused by the whole thing and laughed and said "Bravo", making the matter with Charlesworth even more strained.

At this juncture, I thought it wise to intervene and, picking up the remaining pack, I asked Lawrence if he knew which card would be the next to be drawn. He said that it would be the three of clubs. I turned over the top card and, sure enough, the three. I asked, then, if he might tell me the fourth in the pack. He did so and when I had peeled off four more cards, we all saw that he had been correct. Although the other men clapped and laughed with delight, Charlesworth was almost beside himself and I signalled Nurse Yelland to send for two orderlies. Charlesworth said that he remembered a card-counter in Whitechapel who had been soundly beaten – lucky, according to Charlesworth, to escape death – for practising his skill in the local gambling dens.

I pointed out that wagers at stake in the game at present under way, appeared to be only match sticks but this did not seem to quieten Charlesworth. Lawrence said (and, throughout this speech, he paused for great spaces of time, during which one could practically hear Charlesworth grinding his teeth) that he knew nothing about counting cards but that, over the course of several hands, it had become obvious where each card rested in the pack. Lawrence was not triumphalist, nor was he embarrassed. It was almost as if he couldn't understand what all the fuss was about.

Later, I asked Lawrence if he had known why Charlesworth had become so agitated and he told me that it was probably because Charlesworth could not see where the cards were. He told me he had learned a valuable lesson. I asked him what it was and he simply stared at me for a long time and eventually answered, 'I'm sorry, sir, I'm not sure that I can.' Any other fellow and I should have chastised him for his impertinence but for some reason, I saw little point.

I have seen him essaying sketching and using watercolours but I must report, to no great effect. His skills clearly lie elsewhere. He would be likely to concur, since he seldom seems satisfied with his work and destroys it almost before it is dry.

He continues to spend long hours walking in the grounds - in turns, gazing about him and sitting in apparent contemplation.

I must recount one rather unfortunate encounter. Earlier in the week, I discovered him in the chapel; not at prayer but engaged in what appeared to be close examination of a flickering candle upon the altar. I returned half an hour later and discovered him in the self-same attitude. Asked what he was doing, he merely observed that the candle did not burn! I said that it most certainly did and he asked if I knew what happened to it as it did so. I replied using simple terms and concepts, (which I felt certain he might understand) to the effect that the wax is the fuel, which is drawn up the wick and is burned off by the

flame. The wick is eventually consumed, as is the
greater part of the wax.

He responded that he had once believed that to be
the case but had now determined that neither the
wick nor the wax is destroyed in the process but
that they merely alter their form, becoming heat,
light and vapour, even a very little sound. I was
rather put out that he may have believed that I
didn't know this already and sought to explain that
I had given a simple explanation only in order not
to confuse him. He then blew out the candle and
asked me if I knew where the light had gone. At
this point, I decided that he was making sport of
me and I withdrew.

ITEM: 30/04/15 Letter. Major Dr. James Pennyworth to Sir Maxwell Cavendish

Maj. James Pennyworth

Royal Victoria Hospital,

Netley

Hants.

Friday April 30th 1915

Professor Sir Maxwell Cavendish,

Royal Middlesex Hospital

London W12

Dear Professor,

Captain Stephen Marjoriebanks of the North Derbyshire Fusiliers arrived this afternoon to collect Lawrence. To my shame, I was rather short with him; indeed, I'm afraid I stopped only this side of rudeness.

I had received notice of his arrival, of course, and Lawrence had been informed and he came to say goodbye to me. He was polite, as always but seemed slightly more formal than hitherto. I took it to be my own fancy, since he was dressed in full uniform and looking every inch the soldier. It was rather a shock, to tell the truth, since I had seldom thought of him as such throughout our entire, albeit brief, association. I asked him, as

41

usual, how he was feeling and he told me he was looking forward to returning to his unit. His smile never faltered, of course so I took my reluctance to believe him as emanating more from my own misgivings than from his.

He expressed deep gratitude for the time that both you and I had expended upon him and he particularly asked to be remembered to you. We are, I suppose, getting quite used to this seeming presumptuousness! He told me that he hoped he might have advanced our knowledge and that this might lead to new discoveries about how the brain can recover from frightful wounds such as his own. He gave me a somewhat arch look before adding, "Not than my brain has recovered, quite, eh?" Of course, in spite of my regret at his leaving, training took over and I asked,
"What do you mean, old chap?"
"I believe you know," said he, "More and more becomes visible. I know the world anew each moment and each moment its… (and here, he treated me to a particularly long silence)…song becomes more tuneful and more harmonious. I believe I'm coming to understand *how* this happened but I wonder, doctor, why it happened. Why I know the shape of the world. Why, when so much is visible, yet more is revealed. How much can there be, doctor?"

Then my professional self shook me away and I laid my hands upon his shoulders. With a shake of my head, I told him,

"Why, my dear fellow; I do not know. For I have not one notion of how the world is "visible" to you; how each moment that passes you feel as though you are reborn. Sometimes, I confess, I have envied you your gift. Why, to gaze at the stars and know instantly how many are there, which are fading and which appearing as the world spins. Which will be there and which gone in an hour, a day, a year...a <u>hundred</u> years time! And yet, you have not the words to tell me how it is, nor the wherewithal to show me. I remain in darkness and your world appears to shine."

I'll swear, professor, though he smiled his perpetual smile, there was pity in his eyes. I found I could no longer speak. I was as impotent as Lawrence, himself trying to put into words things that would not allow themselves to be spoken.

XXXX

27 May 1915

Maj. Pennyworth

Royal Victoria Hospital,

Netley

Hants.

Dear Doctor,

Please forgive me if this letter in places displays some of my difficults (*sic*) with expression. It is the thrid (*sic*) draft and I have no more paper. I shall try hard to keep to the matter in hand.

I had to obtain the permission of the Brigadier in order to writhe (*sic*) to you, even though he had in his possesssion (*sic*) the letter from yourself to Major Cresswell. I was flattered that you chose to include a personal letter [to] me in your correspondence with the Major. I would not have missed, for anything, the look on his face his face (*sic*) as he handed it to me. I hope you do not take it from this that I blieve (*sic*) him to be an unkind officer. It is simply that it is so unusual fyr a mansss (*sic*) [*for a man*] to receive a personal letter from an officer. I hope he does not think that I will be getting ideas above my station because of it.

Since you ask, I have been noticing one or two things, which might interest you and Sir Maxwell. I have discovered, for instane, (*sic*) [*instance*] that with the written word, provided I keep each sentence short, I can hold the words the words (*sic*) rater (*sic*) than the visions. They are not visions, of course. They are the things that are. They are the things. They will not let me describe the (*sic*) in words. I have tried to draw them but they are

44

like motes in the eye. The more I try tor ghasp thqm *(sic)*, [*to grasp them*] the further away they fly.

Have you heard of a carillon, Doctor? A carillon it is a marvel that we don't have in England. It is a cunning mechanical system with keys not unlike a piano a piano *(sic)*, which are attached by strings and pulleys. To a number of bells. There is one in the tower here in XXXX. [Loos] It fills the air in the way of our song-thrush in the grounds tree *(sic)* at Netley. Do you still see him, Doctor? Though it has none of the inventiveness of our friend, it being played by a man, a man *(sic)* it is capable of making visible vision visibl *(sic)* and changing the world, although I know what to expect. Those words are feeble. They cannot express what happens when the carillon sings out across the square. At first the carillon, *(sic)* I thought it happened out in the world. Now I know it's inside me. No one else sees. Even I do not see. I don't have visions. I know what the world is truly like when the carillon rings. My own mind, though is trying to help me. This is the second new thing. For now, the visible and the world anew are beginning to sparkle. With colour. It is red, mostly but so many reds many reds *(sic)*! There is a purpose. A purple. Do you suppose this means there might be a blue? I have seen the colours the colours *(sic)* the pattern before in the Botanical Gardens in Sheffield. Aloe Vera. Alow Vera *(sic)*

Forgive me. I read this and it is nonsense. But it is the nearest I have come to using words to explain. You may be able to understand. I sound like a madman and would not send such a letter. But I think it is important. I assure you, though, that I remain content and very much at peace. Safer than I have ever felt, in fact. I do not know why. Know why.

Yours Faithfully,

Private Henry Lawrence.

Autumn 1915

I had done rather well, I thought, in coming through the fighting with barely a graze but all was to change when we briefly gained control of the town of Loos.

Now, in a square in the eastern part of the town, there stood, as is so often the case on the continent, a church tower. Although damaged somewhat, its superior construction had ensured that it remained a valuable vantage point and, indeed, the enemy had been using it as such for a number of weeks, despite our best efforts to flatten it. On pulling out of the town, he had, of course, primed it with explosives and had intended to demolish it.

However, thanks to us, he had left in a bit of a rush and his rear-guard had not been quite so careful as it should have been and had made a rather poor fist of it. The charge failed to go off. I was ordered to take a party from my company of fusiliers to secure the tower, make safe the charges and set up a machine gun as far up the tower as could be. The thinking was to make the best use of it before the enemy had the opportunity to correct his error and send it crashing down with heavy artillery. My own view was that it was rather a foolish manoeuvre and that a single sniper could have been a lot more effective. Our commanders, however, had placed their faith in the Vickers and their plan carried the day.

I selected four men whom I knew to be steady fellows and we set out to follow the order. We were under sporadic fire from a machine-gun about three quarters of a mile to the east but, as yet, the enemy's big guns had been silent. I ordered two men up the tower, to clear a way and to provide any cover they could, whilst two others would follow with the Vickers gun. I would bring up the rear, carrying the ammunition, with the aim of continuing to provide covering fire whilst the gun was set up.

I had barely set foot upon the ladder when a shell struck the tower, not from the east, as we had expected, but from the south. I determined,

47

from the report and from the impact, that it was only a small field-piece and was, strangely you might think, not especially concerned. However, things then rapidly began to get rather sticky.

Another round quickly followed and what felt like a ton of masonry descended upon me and I was knocked out for several seconds. When I came to myself once more, I began efforts to release myself. It was no use. I called up to my men but received no reply. Then a third shell hit, only this time, a little higher up the tower. When the dust had cleared, I gazed upwards and, to my astonishment, saw that the carillon – the bells of the church – was not only still intact but was ringing out as the German machine gun continued to play upon it! It looked as though it would be unlikely to survive another assault by shellfire.

Then, through the murk came a fellow, not from my unit, but one whom I had seen about. His name was Private Lawrence; a strange cove, by all accounts but as bold as lion and, as he flew by me, I called to him,
"There are four chaps up there!" He looked down at me and smiled! "Don't worry, sir, I think I can sort this out," he said and was up the tower like a shot. Every second that passed, I was expecting to be flattened either by the next shell or by the carillon swinging dangerously above me. As it turned out, the next round delivered, mercifully, only a glancing blow. Lawrence reappeared with a man over his shoulder, ran past and was gone, only to return, moments later.

He was still smiling as he ran up the steps once more and smiling as he hurtled down again, another man over his shoulder. Within seconds, he was at my side once more. I protested that there remained two more men but he told me they were dead, as he carefully, almost methodically, removed the rubble from my legs, both of which were broken. He carried me from that infernal tower and laid me in what had once been the cellar of a house. I was in quite a bit of pain and didn't notice him leave. I learned afterwards that he'd gone back up the now crumbling tower, retrieved the Vickers and polished off the machine gun that had been playing merry hell with the bells and my men.

I never had a chance to thank him before I was whisked off to Blighty but he got the D.C.M. for that action and well-deserved.

ITEM: 28/09/15 Citation.

Citation for Gallantry
38th Division 3/16 Bttn. North Derbyshire Fusiliers
Private Henry Lawrence
September 28th 1915

During a prolonged engagement in the town of Loos, during the Battle of the same name, Private Henry Lawrence did act in so gallant a manner that he not only secured the destruction of an enemy machine-gun emplacement but also saved the lives of his Commanding Officer and two of his fellow soldiers. For this act, he is awarded The Distinguished Conduct Medal.

God Save The King!

ITEM: 02/10/15 Newspaper Article

The London Gazette. October 2nd 1915

A FEROCIOUS ACTION!
Enemy Rout!
DCM for Valiant Tommy!

A Report From the Front. By H.L.F. Gregory

Enemy positions had been cleared and the foe had been pushed back to a point about a mile from Loos, a town that he had held for some considerable time. The order was received to press home this advantage and drive the enemy still further from the town. It fell to a small company of men under the command of Captain P.G. Halpern to secure a section of German trench on Hill 70 known as "Old Kent Road". In order to help overcome the ever-present danger of enemy machine gunners who were covering the retreat, Capt. Halpern ordered a two-man team to ascend the belfry of L'Eglise de la Madeleine, which, although having received a number of hits from artillery on both sides, nevertheless afforded still, a vantage point from which enemy positions might be ascertained. As the men above relayed information to their commander below, the church once more came under severe bombardment from German artillery and machine guns.

When it seemed as though the men would surely be killed, Private Henry Lawrence of the North Derbyshire Fusiliers appeared, according to those present, at a full run. Ascending the tower, he recovered a wounded man and helped him to shelter. Still under intense fire, Pte Lawrence returned to the belfry and brought down the second man, who had also received a debilitating wound. Once this man was safe, Pte Lawrence again returned to the building and was able to release from the rubble, Captain Halpern who was unconscious and bleeding

51

from a head wound. Once assured that the Captain was safe, Lawrence returned to the belfry a fourth time and with an extraordinary display of marksmanship was able to silence two of the deadly machine guns. Shells, however, continued to fall.

It is reported that it was only a matter of moments following Lawrence's exit from the stricken building, that the belfry succumbed and fell in ruins.

For this act of extreme bravery and fortitude under fire, Private Lawrence received a citation, as a result of which he was awarded the Distinguished Conduct Medal. The award is to be bestowed by General Rawlinson himself, who will make a special visit to the town for the purpose.

ITEM: 04/10/15 Letter. Maj. Dr. Pennyworth to Pte. Lawrence

Maj. Dr. James Pennyworth
Royal Victoria Hospital,
Netley
Hants.
4th October 1915

Pte. Henry Lawrence
38th Division
3/16 North Derbyshire Fusiliers
France.

Dear Henry,

Congratulations, my dear fellow! All of us here who remember you with fondness were astonished by the accounts we have received of the action at Loos. We are all extremely proud of what you have achieved and I have been given the honour of passing on our gratitude for all that you and your comrades are doing on our behalf.

But you will know, by now, that I cannot allow such an opportunity to pass and so I ask you, if duty allows, to furnish me with as full an account of the action as possible, as you experienced it. What were your thoughts, your motives, other than the obvious, of course. What impelled your actions? How did you overcome your body's natural desire to avoid danger? What were you feeling before, during and after the action?

It may seem callous of me to ask such a thing of you but, as a doctor, I would be failing in my duty to my country and my profession were I not to do so. Please do not believe that I am unconcerned about the effect the action may have had upon you, indeed, I hope to learn something not only regarding the sensations experienced by <u>all</u> soldiers under trying conditions but also upon you in particular. Your actions since your wounding at Ypres have been, I know you will agree, to a large degree out of character with those preceding it. Are you more cavalier with your own safety or, as I suspect, more sure of your ground?

Although you do not seem to believe me, I can assure you that I have no difficulty in understanding your letters. Indeed, the improvement in them is noteworthy.

Once more, congratulations upon your medal, Henry. I of course wish you health and hope that you will be able, as much as possible in your situation, to keep yourself safe until I have the opportunity to speak with you, once more.

My best wishes and my prayers go with you.

Dr. J. Pennyworth.

ITEM: 15/11/15 Letter. Pte. Lawrence to Dr. Pennyworth

XXXX
France
15th November 1915

Maj. Dr. Pennyworth
Royal Victoria Hospital,
Netley
Hants.

Dear Dr. Pennyworth

I thank you for your kind words and for your concern for my well-being. Of course, I cannot doubt your concern for my well-being, as well as your desire to advance your knowledge. Your actions on my behalf, as well as your letters have confirmed me in this believe (*sic*) time and again. I shall be happy to happy to (*sic*) provide as much information as possible.

On the day of the action, I had been with my unit, setting up a defensive line to the east of the church when I saw, above the gunfire gunfire (*sic*) and the occasional artillery shell, the carillon in the tower begin to ring out. I have written to you of the beauty of this machine (which, I will confess, I have found an extremely effecting (*sic*) instrument) but the tones it was producing, now, were of a very different quality. They transfixed me. It appeared, appeared (*sic*) at first, to be a random arrangement of tones (due, no doubt, to the fact that the striking mechanism was inj ther handsd (*sic*) [in the hands] of a machine gunner, rather than a musician!) However, it became vision visible (*sic*) quite quickly that the very randomness itself had a patttern (*sic*) to it.

This told me a great deal about many things. War is chaotic, of course but once the chaos is visible, other things become so. The fallen men were visible but not the wounded. A life in the balance is still a mystery. A great mystery. Not a true silhouette. An outline? A broken battern [pattern?] No. I can't say, for the Officer had fallen beneath the stones and I knew he was not in any danger. The carillon was over him but not like to fall for several minutes. So I left him – he told me to leave him leave (*sic*) and help the men. The dead were gone but the wounded were invisible to me. I found them because they stood out from the carillon. I belive (*sic*) that without it, I might not have found them. I was not afraid except of ricochets, which I couldn't yet understand although I am beginning to.

Destroying the enemy machine gun nest, I did to save my comrades. I do not like to kill. I don't know why. I must do it, though. I don't know why. I am a good shot. I was thinking that those German machine gunners were not aiming at men but at the carillon. For fun. The fieled (*sic*) gunners were trying to destroy the tower, though. I should have tried to silence the gun first but I hadn't the power. I could severely damage the machine guns though and so I did. I killed one man and wounded three. They may die. It is for the best, I think, dreadful as it sounds.

There was only one thing I could have done and so I did it. They didn't deserve to die. I simply cannot explain and when I try, my words, when I read them, are so poorly said. I hope they are of some use to you, Doctor. For the life life (*sic*) of me, I can't imagine why it should be.

Yours sincerely

Pte. H. Lawrence.

Winter 1915 -1916

Professor Sir Maxwell Cavendish
Royal Middlesex Hospital
London W12
20/11/1915

Maj. James Pennyworth
Royal Victoria Hospital,
Netley
Hants.

Dear James,

In reference to your letter of the 14th inst. I quite appreciate your reluctance to include another in our study of Lawrence but I believe that Booth-Carrack may well be able to advance our work significantly.

The drawings you made of the aloe vera plant are an impressive illustration of how complicated patterns can appear in nature and if, as you assert, these are what Lawrence is "seeing", one might conclude that his eye is giving shape to some of the calculations he performs. There is geometry, to be sure and I confess that learning of Booth-Carrack's work on spectroscopy has convinced me that we should at least confer.

He is no medical man so there is much we may keep from him. He need know only that Lawrence's mathematical skills appear to be combining with an (as yet) undetermined alteration of his brain to produce these visions of his. Can it be that he is able to perceive the spectrum but without the need of a refracting prism? Wavelengths of different coloured light, I learn, are able to be calculated. I believe there may be some method upon which our soldier has stumbled that could enable him to do so.

I beg you to give Booth-Carrack the opportunity to meet with Lawrence and then we may best decide how to proceed.

Sincerely,
Cavendish

Capt. John Glendenning,
XXXX
Belgium
26th December 1915

Maj. J. Pennyworth
Royal Victoria Hospital,
Netley
Hants.

Sir,
In response to your enquiry, I have found Private
Lawrence to be an able soldier who has carried out
his duties uncomplainingly and well during the time
that he has been under my command. Apart from the
action to which you refer, he has distinguished
himself upon a number of occasions, which, whilst
not of the same import as Loos, have nevertheless
earned him the respect of the men with whom he
serves. He is an excellent shot – amongst the best
I have ever seen – and the men have often been
grateful for his services as a sharpshooter. I can
recall three incidents when his quick-thinking and
his courage have caused comment and which have led
to my naming him in despatches. One that stands
out for me, was seeing him haul himself over the
parapet, oblivious to the small arms fire to which
the trench is always subject, and retrieve a
wounded comrade, fallen on night patrol. In fact,
he is usually the first to volunteer for night
patrol himself.

I cannot say that his manner of speech has caused
any remark. Although his conversation is of a
somewhat rarefied nature, there are several learned
fellows, who find his company to their liking and,
I would venture, most of the men treat him as a
true comrade-in-arms owing in part, no doubt, to
his optimistic view of things and his ready smile.

I am unable to comment on his writing because I
have been privy to none of it.

There is a matter, which, I own has troubled me,
however. I have recommended he be considered for
promotion to the rank of corporal, a promotion he
has respectfully declined upon two occasions. I
should not like to think that Pte. Lawrence is
unwilling to accept the responsibility of
leadership.

On a related matter, you will forgive my
impertinence if I ask to be allowed to know the
reasons for your request for this information? I
feel certain there has been an oversight since I
should like to think that, should a Senior Medical
Officer feel the need to contact a fellow officer,
albeit of inferior rank, with such a request, he
might consider it a courtesy to confide the
rationale to that officer, particularly if the man
has a condition of which (and for the good of his
men) that officer ought to be made aware.

Yours sincerely,

Captain John Glendenning
North Derbyshire Fusiliers.

ITEM: 21/01/16   Letter.   Col. Gerald McGregor to Sir Maxwell Cavendish

Col. Gerald McGregor,
Snr Medical Officer,
R.A.M.C.

Beaumont Hamel
21st January 1916

Professor Sir Maxwell Cavendish
Royal Middlesex Hospital
London W12

My Dear Cavendish,

I received your letter this morning. In answer to your first question, I am afraid that I am unfamiliar with the work that Dr. Pennyworth has been undertaking with Private Lawrence but I have asked for his papers to be forwarded to me. It seems a most singular case although I cannot yet find it in me to accept the conclusions you say he has reached.

There is evidence, certainly, that major head traumas can result in changes in perception and, indeed, of personality in the patient but one feels that it's quite another matter to claim that any kind of what Dr. Pennyworth terms "enhancement" can have resulted in the case of Pte. Lawrence. Acts of extraordinary courage have occurred all along the Front and it may simply be that Lawrence's time has come, so to speak. Yet again, following his miraculous escape, he may simply feel that his life

61

is no longer his own and that he owes it to God to ensure that what time he has left to him (which may not be very much, judging from the record you enclose) is spent in helping his fellows and his King to victory against the Hun.

Your second question is no easier to answer, I'm afraid. Although we are expecting the Division reinforcements momentarily, no muster rolls have yet been received. I have no reason to expect any change and we may both assume that Private Lawrence will fall within compass of this medical detachment within the week. As soon as he arrives and once Dr. Pennyworth's papers have been received, I shall inform you by telegraph.

However, I have received orders to afford you access to Pte. Lawrence at your convenience and to release him on leave, should you request it.

Please give my kind regards to Lady Frances.

Yours ever,
Mc. Gregor

XXXXX
26th January 1916

Mrs Hilda Lear,
43 Kennet Terrace
Bradfield
West Riding of Yrks.

Dear Mother,

Well, we're here! I am on foreign soil at last and can't wait to get to it. But we have been told that we can write to our families and the boat will take our mail straight back to England. They say you will have it before the week is out. The weather is chilly but we are all very well catered for so don't worry. Our crossing was very rough and lots of the boys were seasick. Considering it was my first time at sea, I thought I did rather well and you will be proud of me when I tell you that I was not sick once! We are pretty done in, I can tell you and we are looking forward to getting to camp. I can't say where as the Officer says it must be kept secret because Fritz sometimes has a go at our ships in the Channel and the post might fall into enemy hands. It seems a bit far-fetched to me but I shan't tell, just to be on the safe side. As I mentioned in my last letter, I am with a really smashing bunch of fellows and you'll never guess one of them who is called Henry Lawrence has been pointed out to me as the same Henry Lawrence that won the D.C.M. last year! The other chaps all say that I should stick close by him in a scrape because he has a charmed life. I do not believe in charmed lives. I will pray each day and trust in God to see me through. His will be done. We have been told to stop now so I will write again as soon as I can.

Your Loving Son,

George Lear

ITEM: 30/01/16 Letter. Sir Neville Booth-Carrack FRS to Sir Maxwell Cavendish

Sir Neville Booth-Carrack FRS
Greystones,
St. Beddes
Cornwall
30th January 1916

Professor Sir Maxwell Cavendish
Royal Middlesex Hospital
London W12

Dear Sir Maxwell,

Sir Neville has directed me to inform you that he will be in London during April of this year and can place himself at your disposal on the 5th of that month.

He will be pleased to receive you in his rooms at the Royal Society at 12 noon.

Yours sincerely

Richard Holden
Secretary.

ITEM: 08/02/16 Communiqué. Lt. Col. Sir Greville Makepiece to O.C. R.A.M.C.

Lt. Colonel Greville Makepiece
Ypres
8th February 1916

Officer Commanding
RAMC 14th Div.
Ostend

It has reached General Plumer that the transport column comprising men of 71st Brigade, casualties of the gas attack at Wieltje, was diverted to Calais on the 4th of this month.

He has been unable to ascertain the reason for this departure from Standing Orders and has asked me to initiate a full investigation. The General is particularly concerned that the column encountered a large contingent of fresh recruits, recently landed at Calais.

I am sure I need not remind you that this deployment of gas on the front line, is designed by the enemy to have a deleterious effect not only upon our forces but also upon morale both here and at home. We should do all we can to ensure that he does not achieve his wish.

Pending investigation, I should like you to ensure that no similar lapses occur and that casualties are despatched to England via Dunkirk with a view to disembarkation at Felixstowe and not Dover, as appears to have happened in this case.

Yours Faithfully,

Lt. Col Greville Makepiece.

Diary of Pte George Lear
6th February 1916

I know it was stupid to have spoken to Sergeant Norris as I did but the chap I was talking to was one of our lads back from the Front. He'd copped some gas and was in a right old state. He told me that he'd just got back off night patrol and was settling down for a kip when he began to hear sounds from further up the line. He said he knew right away that it was gas even though it was the first time he'd seen it because of what he'd heard about it. I could tell he was in a bad way and I am sure that he will die. He was sure, too. The gas gets into your lungs and makes you cough and vomit. This wears off, he said, and you think you're over it but then, after a day, you start to cough up liquid and it becomes hard to breathe. He said it felt like he was under water. And I'd given him one of my cigarettes! He held it between his lips and said it made him feel better. He then told me an address. I think he wanted me to write to someone for him but that was when Sgt. Norris came over and said we had to move away. I was kneeling down to hear better and just turned and said I was going to write down the fellow's address when the sergeant pushed me to the ground with the sole of his boot and said, "You'll do as you're bloody well told!" or words to that effect. I felt awful leaving that poor chap all alone and I can't remember the address he gave me. Even if I could, what would I write? So I'm going before the C.O. in the morning. They haven't locked me up so I don't expect it'll be too serious. I hope they don't dock my pay or Mum will find out and I can't let her know I'm in trouble after only a couple of days.

ITEM: 07/02/16 Court Martial

Proceedings of Courts Martial Middlesex Regiment

Date: February 7th 1916

Name: George Frederick Lear Pte.

President: Lt. Col. W.H. Graceman (7th Buffs)

Members: Captain F.L. Lewes (3rd Royals)

2nd Lt. J.H.C. Pettis (32nd Light)

Charge: That the above named Private Soldier did refuse to obey a legitimate instruction of his immediate Superior, Acting Sgt. A.F. Norris (12th N. Derbys.).

Pleads: Guilty

Verdict: Guilty

Sentence: Confined to Barracks. Three (3) days.

Diary of Pte George Lear
9th February 1916

I received a visit this evening from Henry Lawrence.
It was surprising to me, as he has never even spoken
to me before. I was delighted to see him. CB doesn't
sound like much of a punishment but it means I have to
work hard all day. Even here, there are jobs no-one
wants. I have been cleaning latrines and de-lousing
uniforms of troops further up the line and I have to
sleep here instead of going back to the billet. The
cook says I'm lucky. He got CB for being drunk and
ended up on burial duty although he says it was more a
question of filling sacks with bits of men. I think
he's just trying to frighten me. It has been bitterly
cold all day with a hard frost that never thawed
throughout the whole day. I broke a trenching tool
and the cost of it will come out of my pay but, as
Lawrence said, it could have been much worse.

I was rather in awe of him when he first arrived even
though he is just a Private same as me. I didn't like
to ask straight out how he got his gong and he never
mentioned it at all. He is very self-effacing and not
at all as I imagined a hero to be. But I did ask him
why he had come to see me and he said, with a smile,
"moral support". I believe I know what that means but
was too proud to ask him. He told me that he had
watched me with that chap who'd been gassed and he
quite made me blush in his praise of my actions. I
said I was only doing what anyone would do and he said
something like, (I must try and recall his words
accurately) "When you die, that's it and all about
it." I remember that clearly but then he said, "But
if you don't die straight away, you become unseen."
That wasn't it but it was the gist. I dare say I will
recall his exact words eventually because they seemed
so important. He also said some things about Sgt.
Norris - or "Acting Sergeant" as he insisted on
calling him - that I'd better not write down even
here. But they were said, I believe, more in sorrow
than in anger.

XXXX
25ᵗʰ February 1916

Mrs Hilda Lear,
43 Kennet Terrace
Bradfield
West Riding of Yrks.

Dear Mother,

It has been four weeks since we landed and we have not moved a jot from here. The fellows think we will be boarding a train for the front very soon, which is why they have let us write again because if Fritz does collar our post, it'll be too late for him anyway! I think so, too so I don't think you'll be hearing from me again in a hurry.

We are billeted in a barn owned by a nice old lady called Madam Leclerc who hates the Germans as much as we do. She has family in the east in a town called Verdun and the Huns killed her nephews there and did other things, too which I don't want to go into detail. She tells us to "Keel az many az you can boys!" which I plan to do as soon as I get to the Front.

I hope that you are all well and that dad has got his beans in. Even with all this going on, the farmers are planting here. I saw spuds going in a few days ago and one of our lads was on a charge for pinching a bagful. Everyone says he will be shot for looting but I don't think it can be true. They were only spuds.

Well, I will close now and say, God Bless you all and kisses to the little ones and tell David that unless he gets on and grows a bit we'll have left nothing for him when he gets into uniform. Trust him to miss all the fun!

Goodbye from your son, George.

Spring 1916

ITEM: 01/03/16 Pennyworth's Journal

James Pennyworth
Private Medical Journal

Tuesday March 1st 1916

It appears that Sir Maxwell has persuaded Sir
Neville Booth-Carrack to interview Lawrence. I am
very uneasy about this for many reasons but
chiefly, I am concerned that Sir Maxwell is jumping
to conclusions, since I have never given him to
believe that Lawrence's "visions" have anything to
do with the refraction of light. He has never
mentioned, even in his most rambling letters, the
ability to see a spectrum. He is no fool and would
surely have used the term, had it been so.

Another concern is that Booth-Carrack is, by all
accounts, not a man used to collaboration. Wily as
Prof Cavendish believes himself to be, Booth-
Carrack may have plans of obfuscation of his own.
We are not, after all, mathematical men! The very
fact of his acceptance of Sir Maxwell's invitation
leads one to conclude that perhaps he recognises in
our tale, something that is a commonplace in
mathematics but a deep mystery to the professor and
me. I hope that neither of us comes to regret this.

But even the most cautious and otherwise clear-thinking men of science can be tempted down fanciful paths when something unusual comes along, as in the spring of nineteen-sixteen when I received a letter from that great clinician, Sir Maxwell Cavendish, the Chief Surgeon at the Royal Middlesex Hospital. His particular field of expertise lay in the treatment of head injuries and, since the outbreak of the war, his skills had been in some demand. He was encountering all manner of trauma. The physical injuries were, of course often of novel and astonishing complexity and Sir Maxwell had developed a number of new techniques to deal with them, several of which remain standard procedure in the hospitals of today. Yet there was a particular case, on which he felt the need to consult me.

He had come across a paper of mine, concerning the use of radioisotope tracers in the diagnosis of certain medical conditions. Because of the war, many scientists were no longer able to access the current work on spectroscopy, it being largely German in origin, and so it was felt necessary to add a number of appendices designed to clarify some of the more difficult mathematics. It was one of these, which caught Sir Maxwell's eye and encouraged him to get in touch.

It turned out that he and a colleague, from the Military Hospital in Hampshire, had been following the progress of a Tommy who had had the misfortune to suffer a rifle shot to the head. Amazingly, the man had lived to tell the tale and, (perhaps not surprisingly), had been seeing visions and having delusions ever since. Lately, the delusions had taken the form of his being besieged by vivid colours arranged in precise patterns. He had described these patterns as being quite plant-like in their construction, mentioning in particular, the succulent, Aloe Vera. This, coincidentally, was the same analogy I had used in my paper when attempting to explain the mathematics of certain spectroscopic phenomena.

As I recall, the paper had drawn – at least in part - on notes I had made when, as a student, I had attended a number of lectures given by

Gustav Kirchoff, whose influence can still be seen on even the most current theories, such as those of Shrodinger and Heisenberg and who had postulated the notion that the entire universe may be described as a series of mathematical equations. He had theorised that if the equations governing the myriad wavelengths of light produced by the vibrations of atomic material could be formulated and solved, it would be possible to construct a true visual representation of atoms and molecules.

Moreover, light and form would be the defining feature of any such representation. In other words, the mathematics of the atom might be made apparent as pattern and colour. Of course, no-one alive would be able to make such calculations as rapidly as would be required and the most sophisticated difference engines available to us, even in our own age, are quite incapable of such feats.

Yet, in the view of Sir Maxwell, this Private had developed a gift for the rapid and accurate positing and deduction of complex equations and he asked if it might be possible for a savant such as this to perceive the world in a wholly unique manner; I have to say that I was, at first intrigued. As I studied the notes of the case, I became drawn to the idea that a man might see the world as a series of equations and that those equations might offer an insight into the true nature of reality. "Could this", I wondered, "be the mind that might draw back the curtain upon Kirchoff's imagined world?"

Sadly, the answer became all too apparent all too quickly. The man could indeed perform remarkable mathematical miracles without, apparently, the need for calculation to an extent whereby I was forced to concede that his understanding of mathematics was of a high order. However, he was of an oddly philosophical turn of mind, somewhat inarticulate and (I was sorry to report to the medical gentlemen,) quite mad. I cursed my foolishness in not heeding the inner voice, which had begged me not to respond to Sir Maxwell's request. Fortunately, neither he nor his colleague had made it known to anyone that I was to be involved. Indeed, they themselves, I came to realise, had been working in secrecy and were at least as reluctant as I to endanger reputations on such folly.

It is an ill wind that blows no-one any good, however, and I came away from this encounter with one insight and that is that we should not despair of the ability of human beings of any station in life to comprehend mathematics to a high degree. One would hope, however, that such skill might be obtained through means other than the impact of a rifle bullet upon the cranium.

ITEM: 11/04/16 Pennyworth's Journal

James Pennyworth
Private Medical Journal

Tuesday April 11th 1916

I do not believe we shall hear from Sir Neville again. I am not going to gloat, of course. Prof. Cavendish will be mortified as it is and he will not wish to be reminded how opposed I was to his contacting Booth-Carrack in the first place. I understood him to be a great mathematician and so, I am assured, he is; my mistake was to assume that to be so would demand a degree of intelligence! Thankfully, he had already written me off as some sort of assistant and so we exchanged few words but there were several times, had protocol permitted it, when I would have told him exactly what I thought of him.

His disdain for Lawrence was apparent from the beginning and it was not until the two had spoken at some length that Booth-Carrack was bound to admit that Lawrence understood far more than he could explain. It was not Lawrence's appreciation of the mathematics that was at fault; he merely lacked the terminology to convince Booth-Carrack of the depth of his understanding. It was the first time I fully appreciated Lawrence's struggle with telling how he is experiencing the world.

The mathematician, eventually and I think rather against his will, could understand but, as far as I could see, was able to express himself no better than Lawrence! His own "satisfiables" and "denotational semantics" seemed to me to be more than a match for Lawrence's "visibles" and his "those which are". I should not forget, of course, that we medicos also have our secret language with which we speak to one another. It occurs to me that, were an obstetrician and a farmer to meet, each would likely know as much as the other about animal husbandry; only the terminology might differ.

However, the meetings were not a failure - I must impress this belief upon the Professor when I write - since I suspect Lawrence was able to learn much and whilst the language remains feeble in terms of describing what he experiences, his own understanding has clearly grown. When he left us this time, he thanked us - all of us - for our continued work on his behalf and remarked to Booth-Carrack that now he knew of the Markov chain, the random variables of the stochiastic process had been of tremendous value in understanding the fluctuations of space!

We were all dumbfounded, none more so than Booth-Carrack. Lawrence's parting remark to the mathematician was, "Oh, but Sir Neville, if only you could see the glories they reveal." Booth Carrack said, "Yes, old chap, I'm sure." In so patronising a manner, I wanted to punch him on the nose. When next I meet Lawrence, I shall be curious to see how his analogues have developed. It may be foolish but I hold out hopes that I may yet understand his singular mind.

ITEM: 22/04/16 Lear's Diary

I've only been here a couple of months but I'm beginning to regret my decision to sign up. These entries have become rather morose of late but I am delighted to say that barely a day goes by without me writing at least something down. Not that there is much to write most of the time. We do very little for great long stretches at a time and then, just when we wonder if there really is a war on, either the brass hats or Fritz decide we've had it too quiet for too long and set about reminding us why we're here. There are rumours of a big push coming and it's certainly true that the lines are being reinforced all along the Front. We have ourselves just returned from a long march that saw us well behind our own lines, although we were give no time whatsoever to relax.

I don't know what we were lugging up here, but it was blooming heavy. The "road" such as it was, was deeply rutted and bashed about with shell holes and we had a number of horses go lame and lost no-end of wagon wheels. Sometimes I wonder at what the ordinary soldier is capable of. I would never have thought it possible that such hardships could be endured, before I came here. It may not sound much but a horse swung its head round and caught me across my mouth. Luckily, I lost no teeth but was in severe pain for some time afterwards. Then, a little later, whilst helping to re-mount a wheel, I got a blooming great splinter down my thumbnail. I was hopping but Henry came through, as usual, and yanked it out with pliers.

Then to cap it all, just as we pulled out on the last short haul for the trenches, I found that a stone had got itself inside my boot. Of course, the column could not have halted and so I limped along like I'd been shot. Which is pathetic really because so many men have so much worse happen and there was I mooning over my little injuries. I thought what it must be like to get a piece of shrapnel in the face, never mind a horse's muzzle or, not a splinter but a bayonet in your hand.

I told Henry these thoughts and he said, "Pain is pain, George." And we got to talking about how some men claim that even having been severely injured, they felt little pain at the time.

Henry reckons that some Frenchman in one of the maths books he carries with him decided that everything exists in the mind alone and there is no such thing as sensation. "You're not standing in my boot, are you?" I said. "For if you were, you would soon realise that there is such a thing, I can tell you!"
I laughed and so did he but my foot was becoming quite sore.
"I think, therefore I am," this Frenchman is famous for saying and I fancy I've heard that before but never knew what it meant until Henry explained. I said that if the pain was merely inside my head why couldn't I just stop it by thinking of something else. Henry said that he believed I probably could. He was quiet for a while and then he started going on about our boots being filled with leaves and then with feathers and what have you until he said we should imagine that instead of walking along this hot dusty road, we were paddling through the sea at Bridlington.
At this point, the Sergeant came by and said we were to "pipe down" so we fell silent but I kept trying to will the pain away.
I can't say it worked perfectly but there were long periods when I could tell myself that the stone was something rather more pleasant or even that it was not there at all.
I shall try to remember this should, God forbid, I receive a more serious would although I fancy I'll have too much else on my mind to be able to concentrate.

Captain Charles Hardwicke
1st Wing Royal Flying Corps
Flanders
3rd May 1916

Dr. Caroline Charteris
24 Hanover Square
Mayfair
London

Dearest Carrie,

How on earth have you been? I have had no contact
from you since Paul's funeral. You were obviously
a bit cut up but I'd hoped by now you might have
begun to get in contact with some of your old
friends. I know it sounds a bit harsh, but being
out here forces one to consider the importance of
seizing each moment and, Lord knows, we've all lost
people close to us. I still think of Jimmy and how
we were talking about Christmas leave one moment
and the next – well, you get the picture, old
Carrie, I'm sure. Mustn't dwell and all that.

Anyway, the thing is, I ran into an old pal from
Cambridge the other day in Southampton when I was
over there picking up a kite, name of Pennyworth.
We got chatting, as one does, and it turns out he's
some sort of medico over at the loony bin in Netley
where they send all those "shell shock" cases and
blow me if he isn't in need of a mathematician. I
mentioned your name and he remembers meeting you on
a couple of occasions at Nancy Partridge's place in
Ely. Perhaps you remember him? Tall chap, sandy-
haired, passable tash. He and I were pretty tight
in those days and he really is a jolly good sort.

79

Then swipe me if he didn't ask if I knew how to get hold of you! Who could resist? I told him that you probably wouldn't let me get a hold of you if my life depended on it! He was good enough to laugh but I think he was a bit shocked.

Anyhow, I said I could point him in your direction and told him you wouldn't mind if he wrote but he insisted I clear a path; vouch for his motives and all that. Be a dear, Carrie, old love and drop the feller a line, would you? His moniker and billet:

Maj. James Pennyworth
Royal Victoria Hospital,
Netley
Hants.

Bye for now, old thing and do let's make a day of it next time I'm in town.

Your affectionate pal,

Charlie.

ITEM: 19/05/16 Letter. Major Dr. James Pennyworth to Dr. Caroline Charteris

Maj. James Pennyworth
Royal Victoria Hospital,
Netley
Hants.

May 19th 1916

Dr Caroline Charteris
Department of Mathematics,
University College, London

Dear Dr. Charteris,

It was very good of you to respond so promptly. I
am flattered that you remember me after so few
meetings and after such a time. Charlie told me of
your loss and, of course, I offer my sincere
condolences. This war has made mourners of us all,
I fear. The soldier with whom I would wish to
acquaint you is one of its many victims although,
as you will learn, he has been rather more
fortunate than many. I have enclosed a brief
summary of the facts of his case, which you may
peruse at leisure. Once you have done so, I wonder
if you might do me the great service of
recommending books that may be of interest to the
patient. He is no stranger to mathematics but
wishes to learn more concerning the "language" of
algebra and the calculus. I'm afraid I must
confess that I am no mathematician and have
precious few qualifications that might make me an
effective intermediary but I should add that he is
particularly eager to learn of non-linear
differential equations and turbulence in fluid
motion. Needless to say, I have only the merest
idea of what these are so I find I must place
myself in your hands when it comes to the selection
of pertinent works.

I intend to purchase the books from Hatchards in London but, if you know of any better, perhaps you might inform me as to the addresses.

I do look forward to hearing from you on this matter but, of course, it must be at your convenience. Charlie tells me that your present post keeps you extremely busy so I shall not expect an immediate response. Once again, it is so very good of you to offer to assist me in this matter.

Yours sincerely,

Major Dr. James Pennyworth Esq.

ITEM: 27/05/16 Letter. Major Dr. James Pennyworth to Dr. Caroline Charteris

Maj. James Pennyworth
Royal Victoria Hospital,
Netley
Hants.

May 27th 1916

Dr Caroline Charteris
Department of Mathematics,
University College, London

My dear Dr. Charteris,

How can I thank you? Your parcel arrived not ten minutes ago and I cannot tell you what a surprise it has been. You could not have pleased me more, for the expedition to Hatchards, (though I believed it would be weeks away), was nevertheless, already causing me anxiety. To have that particular cup taken away from me is an extraordinary relief. I shall post the books on to Private Lawrence immediately and impress upon him the enormous generosity you have displayed (although he is a good fellow and is sure to understand with no prompting). I am confident that, as soon as his duty permits, he will be in touch, begging me to pass on his sincere thanks to you, as indeed, once more, do I. I am in your debt.

Yours sincerely,

Major Dr. James Pennyworth Esq.

P.S. I have since discovered your letter addressed to me. I shall read it and reply fully in due course.

J. Pennyworth.

Summer 1916

ITEM: 30/06/16 Orders to Attack

General Orders
issued from the office of
General Baron Henry Sinclair Home GCMG, KCB, KCSI
Cdr. XV Corps.
(Being a précis of same issued by Sir Henry
Rawlinson, General Officer Commanding 4th Army under
instruction from The Earl Haig.)

… 38th Division cont.

14: FORWARD MOVEMENT Zero. First Attack: Forward
Trench all Coy's on whistle. Signal to be given by
Company Commanders as indicated in General Order 1
(ibid). Telephone HQ 05:00-05:30 for
synchronisation All Coy's Officers above rank of
Warrant Officer to lead men AT WALKING PACE. Under
no circumstances must men be instructed or allowed
to break the line. The Field Marshall wishes order
to be maintained throughout the attack.
Communication between Platoon leaders must be
maintained at all times using hand signals and
whistles in the event of smoke. Spotters indicate
enemy defences destroyed by barrage. No sighting
of enemy since 29/06/16.

15: OBJECTIVES   Primary Objective is the capture
of trench systems on Poziers Ridge. No. 4 Coy to
establish machine gun post. A number of sites have
been indicated: a) Top Hat. b) Long Acre. c)
Harcourt Wood. d) Glory Hole Copse. Any of which

will afford line of sight on enemy support and rear trenches.

16: CASUALTIES   Casualties to be ignored until objective is achieved.   Thereafter, signals to be made to bring up medical assistance.   Men may be released at discretion of Coy Cdrs to assist in evacuation of wounded.   No order to retire will be given but, once the objective is achieved, wounded may be withdrawn by all available means.   Support trenches must remain clear for the purpose of evacuation to CCS at Albert.

17: PRISONERS   All prisoners to be passed to the rear accompanied as necessary ten per Private Soldier.   Enemy casualties to be left until such time as Orderlies are available.

18: DISCIPLINE   There will be no throwing of bombs.   Rifles to be presented and no discharge made without express order of Platoon Leader. Enemy targets to be selected at discretion of same. No man shall return to his trench.   All issued equipment must be accounted for once objective is achieved.

20 FEINT ATTACK Zero: "C" Coy to target Hougemont Rd with small arms and mortar fire for 12 minutes. After this time, 147 Machine Gun will open fire: short burst for a further 4 minutes.   Rifle and mortar fire to recommence for 8 minutes.   …cont…

ITEM: 30/06/16 Lear's Diary

```
Diary of Pte George Lear
30 June 1916
```

As usual, no-one has a clue what's going on. The barrage hasn't stopped this past week and we are all heartily sick of it. Not so sick as Fritz though, I'll bet. At least we're only on the noisy end! I can't imagine what those poor souls are enduring. Poor souls. Even as I write that, I find it hard to believe I should feel sympathy for the Germans after what I've seen but I suppose Lawrence is beginning to get to me. He's been a good pal these past months even if he does say some rum things and always at the wrong time. I don't think I'm any nearer to understanding half of what he goes on about but if I have to be here at all, I'm glad I'm with him. Word is that we're going over the top tomorrow. I don't mind admitting that I'm scared but our officers assure us that Fritz's trenches will be in pieces and his wire destroyed. We are ordered to simply walk over no-man's-land and take over the German trenches. I pray that none are left alive for just a machine gun or two could cut our lads to bits. And me, of course. We have been ordered to write goodbye letters to our families but I can't bring myself to do it. God will be with me every step of the way. I cannot doubt that and to write as if I expect to die would display such a lack of faith that I simply cannot countenance it. Lawrence is a fine fellow but I will own up that, as he sits opposite me constantly dripping water from a spoon into a tin cup, with that smile on his face, he is testing my patience. I am likely as not to say something I might regret.

Still, he was very kind about my poem and I think he was quite pleased to have his name in it. He said it was rather jolly. I don't think it's too bad for a first attempt. Some of the lads said I should perform it at the next concert party and one of them said he'd write a tune and we'd sell it to Vesta Tilly! (sic).

People think that the Battle of the Somme was a disaster and it was, for the divisions in the northern sectors but there were some successes. Thank God, our action at Fricourt was one that succeeded. We got as far as the German front lines and I can say with some pride that I actually set foot in a German trench on the day of the Battle of the Somme. There's not many that can. But it wasn't plain sailing by a long chalk. There was not as much damage to the German defences as the top brass had thought and we were raked badly. But I got through the whole thing without a scratch and then, as were clearing up the German trenches, I trod on a picket post and it went right through my foot.

I felt a proper chump being ordered to a clearing station, I can tell you. When I arrived there, I saw Capt. Glendenning who had gone over just ahead of me, lying on a stretcher. His arm was covered in blood and it looked pretty bad.

'Greaves,' he says, 'are you hurt badly?' That was typical of him. He was always concerned about his men. 'No, sir,' I said. 'I trod on a picket.' I was bit worried, you know, because some chaps would do that sort of thing to get sent home and there were some as were shot for that but he just laughed. As it turns out, his wound wasn't as bad as it looked and he was up and about in a few days. One fellow by the name Henry Lawrence – lucky as ever, he was – had his tunic fairly shot to ribbons but not a shot touched him! Full of holes! It was all about good fortune, d'you see; whether you made it through or not.

The Devonshires were wiped out, of course. Major Martin of the 9th Devonshires had reccied the battlefield to such an extent that he knew every German machine gun in the area. He'd told his commanding officers, you know and he'd even built a model of the landscape out of plasticene to show how the German guns could hold the line. They didn't listen o' course and the Devonshires copped it badly.

If you go there today, you'll find the cemetery there, where the trenches were and there's a piece of old board that says on it 'The Devonshires held this trench: they hold it still.' Very moving. Very moving.

ITEM: 12/07/16 Letter. Pte. Lawrence to Dr. Pennyworth

12th June 1916

Maj. Pennyworth
Royal Victoria Hospital,
Netley
Hants.

Dear Doctor,

I am very sorry to have to report a mishap, which has befallen one of the books you sent me. The translation of Sir Isaac Newton's Principia Mathematica - which has been a constant companion since first I opened it - has been mutilated.

When we went over the top at Fricourt, it was struck by a machine-gun bullet, which passed through the pocket of my tunic as I turned to avoid it. It was a foolish error. I am constantly aware, as I have tried to explain to you before, of everything that is around me. Indeed, I find the limit of that awareness increasing each day. If I am able to sense - in the common manner of the word - I find I understand not only the whereabouts but the relative positions in time and space of that which I sense. Some things are simply too far away but I am finding it more usual to postulate based upon my understanding of that which is nearer to me.

Thus, I was nonplussed to find that I had failed to prevent the tail of my tunic swinging into the path of the projectile. I have enclosed with this letter, a note to Dr. Charteris expressing my deep regret at the loss of so marvellous a thing. As soon as I am able, I shall, of course, replace it. I regret, too any embarrassment I may cause you by my stupidity.

I also apologise for not contacting you sooner. This is the first opportunity we have had to

compose letters since July 1st.   They are to be
sent this evening.
Doctor, be proud of me.   For the first time, you
are to receive the <u>first</u> draft of a letter.   I have
read it and it seems not to have been written by a
madman.   I owe you so very much!

Pte. Henry Lawrence.

ITEM: 25/07/16   Letter. Sir Maxwell Cavendish to Major Dr. James
Pennyworth

                   Professor Sir Maxwell Cavendish
                      Royal Middlesex Hospital
                           London W12

                                           25/07/1916
Maj. James Pennyworth
Royal Victoria Hospital,
Netley
Hants.

Dear James,

I shall come straight to the point. I fear I
cannot support your view in the matter of Lawrence
and the incident with the book. My own view is
that Lawrence's brain injury may have left him far
more damaged than we at first believed. I
witnessed the savantism first-hand, of course and I
do not doubt that the impact is likely to have been
the cause but it is a great distance from feats of
calculation to evading a machine gun bullet!

I am left to conclude, therefore that poor Lawrence
is now subject to strange and obviously dangerous
delusions. I would conjecture that his decoration
for valour and his good fortune, thus far at least,
on the field of battle have caused him to suspect
that he is now invulnerable. In searching for a
reason, his fevered mind is telling him that it is
his gift that has been the key.

As you have often told me, dear boy, I am no
psychiatrist but even I could not help but note
how, in his letter to you, he announces his super-
human ability in the form of a mere passing
mention; as though it were of so little import that
explanation is not needed.

                           92

I remember visiting the Bethlehem Hospital and being introduced to a fellow who claimed to be the King. He too was so utterly convinced that he began speaking to me as though it were perfectly natural that he should find himself in a padded room! He even spoke of remembering me from the time he bestowed my knighthood!

I beg of you, James, tell no-one of your precipitate conclusions. As your friend, I can forgive you this lapse – particularly as I know how convincing Lawrence can be – but there are many who would not. Indeed, if psychiatry is anything like medicine, there will be those who would be delighted to see you make a fool of yourself.

I have returned Lawrence's letter as requested but would strongly advise that you merely place it in a file of psychiatric curiosities and pursue the matter no further.

Prof. Sir Maxwell Cavendish.

ITEM: 01/08/16 Letter. Dr. Caroline Charteris to Maj. Dr. James Pennyworth

Dr Caroline Charteris
Department of Mathematics,
University College, London

1st August 1916

Maj. Dr. James Pennyworth
Royal Victoria Hospital,
Netley
Hants.

Dear Dr. Pennyworth,

Thank you so much for forwarding the letter from Private Lawrence. He tells me that he has informed you of the damage caused to my poor *Principia*! You must tell him, as have I by private letter, that it is of no matter whatever. Indeed, I have already sent him a replacement copy – I have been through a number of them since I was a student and I have sent one of the least dog-eared! I was intrigued by his remarkable account of how the mishap occurred. It sounded most dramatic. It is difficult for those of us left behind to appreciate the terrors to which our troops are exposed daily.

I wonder, Dr. Pennyworth, whether you, yourself have experienced battle? My dear, late husband (killed in the self same Battle of Ypres where Private Lawrence received his own injury) gave me several vivid accounts and even allowing for his preserving me from the worst of it (as I do not doubt he would have), I could scarce imagine how anyone might emerge unscathed from such a thing. Which brings me to Private Lawrence's equations.

As you have mentioned, his command of written language leaves a little to be desired and I understand this is one of the consequences of his injury. However, I can assure you that his command of the language of mathematics is of a magnitude I have seldom seen. At first, I was unsure of what I

94

was seeing. It was as though, frustrated by his inability to express himself in words and realizing suddenly that I might understand, Private Lawrence had fallen into describing his experience in the form of equations and postulates. It took me several readings and a number of hours with my books but, if I understand correctly, I believe that, in the guise of a common soldier, you may well have a genius on your hands.

Tell me, has he ever spoken to you of Planck or Einstein? They are German mathematicians who have been demonstrating, with some success, how advanced mathematics can explain the most fundamental elements of the physical world. There is nothing so contemporary in any of the works he now has in his possession. Of course, he may have acquired a teacher who has explained matters to him but (and, I'm afraid you must take my word for this, for to prove it would take several pages of calculus) Lawrence's workings do not bear the characteristics of either Planck or of Einstein.

I realize that it is rather presumptuous and you are no doubt extremely busy so you will understand how important I believe the matter to be if I ask that you might receive me at Netley for the purpose of discussing the case more fully. I can be contacted at the above address, of course but a telephone call to my secretary, Miss Griggs, on Bloomsbury 183, is likely to expedite matters. I shall make myself available to leave at short notice, so you need not concern yourself with my convenience.

Yours sincerely

Caroline Charteris.

                                    Caroline Charteris
                              Department of Mathematics,
                              University College, London

                                    September 22nd 1916

Maj. Dr. James Pennyworth
Royal Victoria Hospital,
Netley
Hants.

I should like to thank you and your staff for the hospitality afforded me last week-end on my visit to Netley and for the opportunity to exchange ideas. In this, I fear I may have had the better of the bargain! I sensed at our parting that you were possibly rather more confused than had been the case before we met and my frustration at my own inability to make myself understood may also have shown itself.

For this, naturally, I apologise. As natural philosophers - to use the antique but accurate term, we sometimes forget that our own field can be a closed book to many, even to those who are masters of their own. Disciplines may often contradict, as much as complement, I am sure you will agree. Had our conversation concerned the complexities of the mind or indeed, of the physical brain, I dare say that it would be you writing to me at this moment.

However, on the train journey up to London, I began to consider how I might better express to you what I imagine Private Lawrence is experiencing. I shall not use my abstractions, my determinism and my three-body postulates but shall (as indeed does Lawrence himself), attempt to describe and explain using analogy. Do not, I pray, believe that I hold you to be incapable of a deeper understanding. It is simply the case that Private Lawrence's new native tongue has been my own for more than half my life; therefore, I offer my services as translator.

Imagine, if you would, that you are a novice rail passenger. Indeed, you have never before travelled at speed. Now, imagine the train journey from your own delightful and bucolic Netley to my own grey, fevered London.

You board in familiar surroundings, perhaps seen off by a charming companion with whom you have spent a fascinating day and, as you take the seat that will be yours for the next few hours, the train begins to move. You glance out of the window and, even as the train picks up speed, you are yet able, (true; perhaps from an unfamiliar vantage point), to identify features with which you are familiar; that elm, those cottages, the chalk-flecked hills and, glimpsed through a cleft in those same rolling downs, the sea; green, almost inviting.

As the train speeds along, the landscape begins to take on a rather less comfortable aspect for not only do you no longer recognize what you see, but also, the image beyond the window is now no more than a blur. Was that an oak? Perhaps an ash? It was a tree, certainly; of that, you are sure. A pond, a river? No; merely a field of blue flax. Are those men in the field using spades or hoes? Are there rabbits or simply tussocks of rough grass? How could anyone tell at this speed? By now, you are somewhat bewildered. You are sure that outside, the landscape is static and the people are going about their business at their normal leisurely pace and yet to you, their actions and their situations are little more than a mere jumble of colours, textures, patterns that flicker and dance and change beyond your mind's capacity to sense clearly.

And so you draw your gaze inside the carriage and now all is clear, all is calm and all is comprehensible. You take up your Times and you begin to attempt the crossword. Gradually, the frenzy beyond the glass is forgotten and you and companions with you in the compartment are, to all intents and purposes, your world.

Now something once more draws your attention to the scene outside. The train has entered a region of open marshland. Gone is the chaos and, in its place, a sense of things slowing down. The train, though, continues at its original pace but because you now have distance between you and the objects in the landscape, you can focus once more. Yes, a beech tree; a cart and there: some sheep! Now you see. But too quickly, the landscape closes once more and, with a start, the frenzied tapestry returns. Perhaps your memory retains still the sight of that tranquil scene; even now many hundreds of yards behind. It is there – you know it is – but it is gone from your sight.

And now what is this? Deceleration; you are eased forwards, gently in your seat and the blur beyond the glass is coalescing once more into a different, yet somehow familiar, picture. The trees are no longer strips and blotches of grey and green but have bark and boughs, knots and leaves. Leaves you have always known they had, even as they flew by at speed but now, you can see them. You might even be able to see an individual leaf and if you are fortunate and the evening sunlight falls through it, you may even fancy that you can identify the veins running through its translucent body. This leaf is the protoplasm, which, when subject to the velocity of the train, formed the green splash that had accompanied you these many miles. And yet, until you were at rest, it was invisible.

Then (and here you may appreciate some of what Lawrence is going through) imagine if others in the compartment were unable to see the leaf, the tree, the cattle and the sheep. Imagine that, to everyone else, there was only the blur. How, then, might you explain the leaf?

Now, Doctor; let us say that you are Private Lawrence hurtling along through life with the rest of us. Suddenly, your headlong rush, relieved only by the occasional clearing, so to speak, comes to an end; gradually at first until eventually you are moving slowly enough to see more than the blur. As you stop at last, why, there … there is the leaf. In other words, the actual constituents of a world whose parts others may posit or can even <u>prove</u> exist but which none, save you, can perceive.

I fear, with the preceding paragraph, I may have "de-railed" my own analogy! I should not be surprised, since most analogies tend to break down eventually. Yet I shall persevere.

Have you, Doctor, ever watched a child playing catch-the-ball? It is, I submit, a true wonder. How so? Because the child who catches a ball thrown by another is demonstrating that his body and his brain are capable of breathtaking mathematical and geometrical calculations of which his common understanding is entirely ignorant.

Consider: his eye watches his partner's hand swing away from him to a certain point in space where, momentarily, it stops. The hand then begins to move forwards, possibly (although not necessarily), retracing the same arc. At some point, the child sees the other's hand relax its grip on the ball and his attention instantly switches from the hand to the ball itself. The ball, for a few moments, accelerates at a tangent from the original arc of force and then under gravity, it takes on a parabolic trajectory.

Before the ball has reached the apogee, the child's hands have begun to move upon a course that will allow them to intercept the ball at a place it has yet to reach. A split second before contact, the child's hands slow down and the ball is taken. But the miracle is not yet complete. For now, the hands may travel onwards and lift the ball so that it might fall into the palms of his hands or else they might even reverse their previous course and, cushioning the momentum of the ball, bring it to rest.

At any point from start to finish, an infinite number of possibilities are conjectured. All, (and here you must take my word for it) are as likely as not to occur. The child takes account of all these possibilities faster than it is possible to think – predicting, if you will, where the ball will be at any given moment.

So, you see, if even a child can do these things, literally without active thought, does it not suggest that all men have the inherent capacity to perceive the world in a manner beyond that which we usually term "sense"?

I am prepared to posit that Lawrence has begun to see the world as a series of complex, yet subtle and, no doubt, beautiful equations, some of which he has written down for me and which, you will recall, I failed utterly to explain to you. The chaos we observe in our world is, to Lawrence, as predictable as the trajectory of a thrown ball. He performs no calculations, as we might understand them; he merely knows that which is, under any given set of circumstances.

I do not, I assure you, have the faintest idea what form his perception takes – it is simply, literally beyond my understanding but the tale of the song-thrush and Lawrence's interest in fluid dynamics may offer some insight. For, at some level, I believe that Lawrence is able to "see" the song of the thrush. As the waves of sound alter the very molecules of the air around it, it must take on … I know not. I suspect that he perceives the minute changes in air density with his eyes much as we perceive them with our ears. Consider how, at Loos, the wounded men were "seen" against the sound of the carillon.

His mention of aloe vera may be pertinent. This plant, as I'm sure you are aware, is sometimes cited as evidence for the existence a Creator God since it appears that none save a conscious being could devise the wonderful complexity, combined with regularity, which it exhibits. And yet it grows, as all plants must, chaotically. This, of course, is why (although all specimens are similar), no two can attain, nor can they ever display, exactly the same configuration. It is, I assure you, theoretically possible to determine the point at which each individual plant diverged from its fellow in its pattern of growth. This is not how God but how Nature manipulates the universe. There are patterns to chaos and, I am coming to believe, Henry Lawrence perceives them.

And now, I call upon your expertise, dear Doctor Pennyworth. Firstly, is it possible for anyone to determine the purpose of that damaged portion of Lawrence's brain? With what aspects of understanding is it believed to be concerned? Secondly, I wonder if you have heard of anyone, mad or otherwise, claiming to be able to "see" sounds? In addition to considering these questions, I should be most interested to hear what you make of my ramblings.

Although I assure you that they are based upon the sound and accepted work of a small but well-respected group of mathematicians, I realize that they must seem quite bizarre. I long for the opportunity to test my conjecture. When is Lawrence due home on leave? I dearly wish to meet him in person.

By the by, I believe that Sir Neville Booth-Carrack may have made a very significant mistake in dismissing your Tommy. I shall send you an abstract of a work by Gustav Kirchoff, which describes a world that is nothing but mathematics and which, he

101

believes, it is only a matter of time before we will possess the wherewithal to perceive. I cannot believe that Booth-Carrack does not know this work. He may come to regret his prejudices.

Goodbye for now, Dr. Pennyworth. I do so look forward to receiving your thoughts on these matters. Until I have the pleasure of your company once more, I remain

Yours sincerely,

Caroline Charteris.

ITEM: 30/08/16 Letter. Major Dr. James Pennyworth to Dr. Caroline Charteris

Maj. James Pennyworth
Royal Victoria Hospital,
Netley
Hants.

August 30th 1916

Dr Caroline Charteris
Department of Mathematics,
University College, London

Dear Dr Charteris,

I was so pleased to receive your letter of the 22nd. I must confess that I too felt that our meeting ended a little uncomfortably. My thick-headedness must have been terribly trying for you and I cannot apologise enough. You certainly did not get the better of the bargain, though, I assure you. For my part, I spent several hours in the company of a woman of charm, intelligence and wit, whilst you spent the afternoon trying to make a silk purse out of a particularly dull sow's ear!

In answer to your first question regarding the functions of the brain, studies of patients who have survived brain injury have led to a number of assumptions regarding the possibility that thought, movement, personality and so forth may be controlled by different regions of the organ, although it is widely accepted that we are many years from developing any deep understanding of how the brain functions. As yet, only our Creator knows for certain and, for the present, He keeps that knowledge hidden from us. Perhaps with good reason.

As to your second question, however, there may be an answer extant. Although I shall need to verify this, a colleague of mine, here at the hospital, tells me of a condition of which he knows little save the name. It is called synaesthesia. As the word would suggest, it refers to the capacity demonstrated by some individuals, to sense the same stimulus in more than one way. Thus, a person would experience a sound and the sensory response might be a combination of the mundane (i.e. audible) and the less so, for example, a sight or even a scent. Imagine a musical note whose effect one could smell or see as well as hear! Certainly, if Lawrence (as you have hinted) somehow "sees" a sound, it might lend credence to the contention that he could discern patterns in the movement of the air.

This entire notion excites me and I long to learn more but, at present, it is impossible. There is so much to do here and in two weeks' time, we are hosting an important conference on the diagnosis and treatment of shell-shock. We hope to convince military commanders that it is a very real and debilitating condition, which requires treatment rather than punishment.

As soon as I am able, I should like to take myself off to the British Museum Reading Room to study. It will be so welcome an occasion that I might even take it as a sort of holiday. In which case, I should be honoured if you would consent to accompany me on an outing - perhaps to the theatre or a concert, followed by dinner at my club.

Should you agree in principle, perhaps you might ask Miss Griggs to drop me a line and let me know. It would certainly lend my decision to come to town a little more urgency, were I to know that I should have the pleasure of your company for an evening.

Yours Sincerely
James Pennyworth.

Autumn 1916

ITEM: 30/10/16 Letter. Pte George Lear to Parents

Ypres,
Belgium
30th October 1916

Mr and Mrs John Lear,
43 Kennet Terrace
Bradfield
West Riding of Yrks.

Dear Mother and Father,

At last, I have the opportunity to write to you! A change of scene for us. Because of our success at Fricourt, we have been sent to help out our lads who are holding off the Germans at the town of Ypres. All the lads call it "Wipers" because they can't get their tongues around the names, here. You would laugh because some of the towns have such funny-sounding names here where there is some French spoken but mostly Belgian.

There is White Sheet and Plug Street and Poppy Ring (or just "Pop") and a lovely one, I think, called Passion Dale. The country is very like northern France and before Fritz got here there were lots of farms and little towns but he has flattened the lot.

The soil is really good here, though dad. After the war, you should think about coming here to farm. No hills and no moorland so Old Jenny could retire and we'd get one of those little broad-shouldered Belgian beasts that they all use here. But I don't expect you'd want to leave the crags, which are, I will admit, a lot more interesting than here. I long to stand on Scarsdale, once more; the wind in my hair and the warm sun on my face. Listen to me. I've become quite the poet!

The food is better here even though there are Germans all around and this is why they want Ypres, of course because of the good roads and the train lines, which run practically all the way to Blighty. Well, we'll hold it, if it means our dinner and letters from home and cakes and so on! I still miss you all and long to see you again. I was very pleased to hear that our David got his scholarship. He should not even think of coming here until he has finished his studies. He might end up an officer and be my commander! Wouldn't that be a lark?

Don't worry about me. I am fit and well and, as my great chum, Henry Lawrence says, "Bullets don't have your name on them, old fellow, just numbers!" He is quite the card sometimes.

God bless you all and I will write to you soon.

Your son

George Lear.

ITEM: 30/10/16 Lear's Diary

Ypres October 30 1916

Today had the smell of Winter on it. We've been in the Salient for three weeks now and, as the Fifth Army on the Somme is brought to strength at last, it looks like we'll be here for some time. Lord, I thought the Somme was hell but it was mere purgatory compared to this place. Lawrence was here for the First Battle and he says it's even worse now than it was then. At least, he says, there were some visible routes within and approaching the town; whereas now, there is little to distinguish the centre of Ypres from the filthy wasteland that surrounds it. The pity is that this country is so fertile and full of promise but millions of shells have literally turned the place inside out so that fetid clay has been brought up from the depths and, for now, the goodness of the soil is interred beneath it. I pray that we have a dry winter, for the water-table appears to be so close to the surface that it will not take much to have us permanently under water.

Fritz is on three sides of us and we run a narrow gauntlet through to the west of the town and the relative safety of our lines. Any movement eastwards, north or south is little short of suicide and yet infantry is called on to make these journeys three times a day to relieve and reinforce the trenches. Tomorrow, we are to provide cover at Hellfire Corner. Pray God my wits remain sharp.

I almost forgot to include the thing for which I took up my pencil in the first place! Just out of reach of the German guns is a little town, west of Ypres called Poperinghe. The lads, of course, call it "Pop" and it has gone pretty much unscathed these last thirty months. The locals have been very enterprising and practically the entire town seems devoted to the comfort and pleasure of the British soldier.

There is one wonderful place, that we call "Toc H" or Talbot House, where officers and men mingle and mix as though there were no division whatsoever. They run concert-parties there and Lawrence and I went to see one last evening. I was disappointed that it wasn't a variety show with some good old sing-a-longs and knock-about comic routines but rather some highbrow stuff with a violin and a piano. What's more, it was to be a selection of modern music so I felt doubly aggrieved but, since entertainment of any kind is so rare, we went along.

It was surprisingly well attended and, I must admit, I enjoyed the music. It was by Gustav Holst, Frederick Delius and Ralph Vaughn-Williams and was played very well indeed by two officers from the Corps of Music, one on the violin, the other on the piano. It was the finale - a Vaughn Williams piece I enjoyed the most called "The Lark Ascending". I would swear he manages to capture the soaring quality of a skylark to a "T" with trills and high notes, which, as I closed my eyes, fairly flung me back to Bradfield Moor where larks jump out of every thicket on warm summer mornings.

At some point, I opened my eyes and noticed Lawrence staring across the aisle at a young Canadian Officer who was swaying back and forth in time with the music. The music was very reminiscent of England and many a man had a tear in his eye but, within minutes, this fellow's eyes were filled with them and his mouth was agape, as he stared, wide-eyed at the violinist.

As the final notes died away and the applause began, the chap slumped in his seat, engulfed by sobs. He was clearly there alone because no-one went to comfort him. Indeed, I imagine his distress caused something of a rush to clear the tiny hall. Soon there was no-one left save this young Officer, Lawrence and myself.

110

I have mentioned often enough in this journal, Lawrence's numerous peculiarities and his sympathetic nature so I was unsurprised to see him move to sit beside the fellow. As he did so, the young chap began to draw himself together and he quickly regained composure. Lawrence said to him,

"What do you see?"

The Officer looked very hard at Lawrence and, finally, he asked,

"You see them too, don't you? When I was young, I thought everyone could see the colours. It is only as I have grown older that I realise it is not the case. Usually, I can control the emotion but that piece is remarkably effective at conjuring the patterns."

Lawrence said,

"They are there, of course but tell me, is that all you see?" The Canuck gave Lawrence a puzzled frown and said something like, "Is it not enough?" Lawrence then said something to him, which I simply cannot recall. It must have been something mathematical; from one of his books, I suppose. The chap looked at him in utter bewilderment.

Lawrence sighed, stood up and laid his hand on the Canadian's shoulder and said to him, "Tell me, is it a gift or a curse?"

"Something of both", he replied.

As we left the hall, Lawrence said to me,

"He is very lucky, for he sees only the light and not the dark."

I knew there was no point in asking him to explain. Whenever I have done so and he has tried, he has always failed.

Winter 1916 -1917

ITEM: 01/01/17 Letter. The Hon. Charles Hardwicke to Dr. Caroline Charteris

```
                              Charlie Hardwicke
                     Royal Victoria Hospital,
                                       Netley
                                       Hants.
                                  1st Jan 17
```

Dr. Caroline Charteris
24 Hanover Square
Mayfair
London.

Dearest Carrie,

A Happy New Year to you, old thing! Happy indeed! For, here I am, still in the land of the living (no thanks to Fritz) and a couple of stone lighter into the bargain! James will have told you all the circs, I'm sure so I'll not go on but I want it known to all and sundry of my acquaintance that, despite some reports to the contrary in certain rags which shall be nameless, I DID NOT CRASH! I landed perfectly, as befits one of my grit and determination. I was limping away when she went POOF! So I remain as transcendently beautiful as ever I was. You will still love me, I am certain of it!

I am in no pain that a goodly dollop of morphine (and a sly Scotch when Nurse Harries is distracted) can't whisk away in a trice but am heartily sick of lying here – view of garden and of Nurse Harries notwithstanding – beneath this sort of hangar thing that keeps the bedsheets off my poor old stump. I ask anyone who looks remotely capable of complying to heave me up so that I might at least totter to the privy rather than use this sorry arrangement upon which, even now, I balance precariously.

Now, don't make that face. As a cripple, I am allowed to discuss my lavatory with whomsoever I choose and I choose you, my sweetheart. Are you not glad of it? James comes to see me every day and I rather get the impression that you and he are become (how might I put this without playing the boorish soldier?) rather more than mere colleagues.

I do hope not. I should die if he stole you from me! To lose you once was unfortunate enough – as the Bard says – but to lose you twice would be careless indeed. Oh, who am I kidding? We both know that you are simply not good enough for me! I deserve a countess at the very least. Don't you think?

In all seriousness, Carrie, old love, I hope that you and James can come to some sort of terms. A more perfect couple I cannot imagine! There, I have said it and, as a war hero and bona-fide wounded soldier, I may not be chastised for my candour!

Anyway, rest assured that I shall not let this little mishap get the better of me. As soon as I can strap on a peg-leg, I'll go and see if I can't get one back for the home side. Brandywine, my mechanic assures me it is but a matter of moments to set up the Bristol to accommodate my new status and I expect to be looking down on his shiny bonce before the snow melts!

I notice that Nurse Harries is beginning to doze in her chair so I think it may be time for my (ahem) medication. Strike whilst it's hot!

Love and kisses to you (and, of course, to the lovely Miss Griggs) and if the mood takes you, I'll wager James will be as delighted to see you as I should, if not (you sly pair) even more so.

All the best to thee and thine,

Charlie

```
                              Dr. Caroline Charteris
                               24 Hanover Square
                                          London
                               January 4th 1917
Squadron Commander Hardwicke
The Royal Military Hospital
Netley
Hampshire
```

My poor, dear Charlie,

Words simply cannot express the sorrow I felt at hearing of your "mishap" as you called it. Trust you to make light of such an awful thing. My only consolation is that I know you are in very good hands indeed.

Of course, I shall be along to visit you presently, as soon as they tell me you are up to it and if your letter is anything to go by, that shouldn't be too far off. In fact, I was extremely cheered to see that you appear to have lost none of your good humour, for a positive outlook is extremely strong medicine, as no doubt you are aware.

Do not take this, however, as a sign that I approve of you dosing yourself with whisky. It is very foolish of you to do so when taking morphine. No small wonder that you seem so jolly but certainly, James tells me that, in his experience the men who think positively and do not despair of their circumstances, are sure to fare much better than those for whom the mental anguish is very great.

I have no doubt in my mind that I shall shortly be hearing of your exploits in the skies soon enough but please, for me, make sure that you are fully repaired before you go flying again. You've only got the one spare now; don't forget!

All my love,
Carrie

ITEM: 13/02/17   Letter.   Dr. James Pennyworth to Dr. Caroline Charteris

Maj. James Pennyworth

Royal Victoria Hospital,

Netley

Hants.

13/02/17

Dr Caroline Charteris

73 Hanover Square

Mayfair

London W

Dear Caroline,

It was such a bore that I had to say goodbye to you so abruptly last Thursday. I should have liked very much to stay for tea but Lawrence and I were both committed to being at Netley before eight o'clock and, as I believe I mentioned at the time, I had no idea where the time went!

How kind you were to my wounded soldier and how you listened! He is considerably less obtuse than when I first met him but when you and he were in conversation, I couldn't understand a word _either_ of you said! And yet, I believe, you understood him perfectly. Certainly, he wished me to pass on to you, his deepest appreciation for the time you had given him and, to which I add my own.

I was particularly impressed that you recognised the drawings as being some sort of ocular device as so it has proved. I handed them to one of our laboratory technicians, here, who recognised it as a rather sophisticated (in his view) range determining device. I asked if it might be made from the drawings and learned of a fine ship's chandler, in Southampton, who might be able to engineer it. I shall take the drawings down there at the earliest opportunity. I rather suspect Lawrence may be able to assist in the war effort after all!

Fortuitously, I shall be in town again, next week – Friday 23rd. I wonder if we might meet at Claridge's, once again? Although, if you are concerned about running into Lady Frances, we could try elsewhere! It is too unkind of me, for she is a very dear Lady but it was rather awkward, wasn't it? Unless I hear to the contrary, I shall book a table and send a cab around for you at eight.

Yours,

James

ITEM: 14/03/17 Letter. Cpl. Lawrence to Dr. Pennyworth

Ypres
14th March 1917
Maj. Dr. Pennyworth
Royal Victoria Hospital,
Netley
Hants.

Dear Doctor,

This is a truly awful place. I am surrounded by
death and by destruction on all sides - quite
literally - for the Germans are making every effort
to pinch the western fringes of the salient and
encircle us entirely. And, yet, for all the
horror, I remain content, happy, even. The enemy
will never capture this town, I am certain. And,
as you know by now, when I am certain, then I am
indeed certain!

The future is not in the stars, Doctor; it is in
the mathematics. I have equations in my head that
make me privy not only to what truly is, but also
to what might be. As each moment passes, the
possibilities fall away, leaving probabilities,
then likelihoods which themselves surrender to
certainties.

I wonder if you shall ever appreciate just how much
you have done? The books, I think, were the
pivotal point. Understanding the mathematics has
cleared my mind wonderfully.

It is as though one had been living in a fearfully
untidy room, awash with papers, thick with dust and
surrounded by so much detritus that one cannot even
begin to decide which bit to clear first. But now,
everything is tidied away, the papers are all in
order and the room is as clean as a new pin! When

the odd mote lands, one is able, with little effort, to dust it away.

I have been considering how I might use these new-found skills to assist the war effort. Although I remain convinced that militarism should be opposed, I am beginning to realise that there is more than one way, if you will forgive the expression, to skin a cat. Our own Generals remain several miles from the front lines they are controlling and the German warmongers who are responsible for all this in the first place, are conducting their war from Berlin. As it becomes easier for me to spot and kill German soldiers, so I become less inclined to do so, for they are as much victims as we.

As I told you in my last letter, Captain Glendenning has promoted me to Corporal and, although I am far from sanguine about it, I realise that it may afford me a number of opportunities to discover the extent of my abilities. Already, my sharpshooting has gained me the use of an elephant gun but, alas, my orders usually call for me to kill soldiers – other sharpshooters, in the main. Nevertheless, up to about eight-hundred yards, it can disable a machine gun, most small field pieces and can even (at much closer range, of course) punch through armoured steel.

If I can, I try to damage materiel rather than men but I continue to kill and my own comrades continue to die. Do not worry, though; I have not forgotten your advice. I know what it means to disobey a direct order. Many is the time I have watched men walk to certain death knowing that I could have warned them. Yet, on second thought, what good would it have done? They could not have not *(sic)* have refused to go.

Imagine, Doctor, if you could see could see *(sic)* the approach of a motor car and, some yards away, a small child running into the road and be unable to convince the child that unless he moves more quickly, or does not move at all, the car and he will surely collide. I see the approach of disaster as clearly as that. To you, one car and one child on an intercepting trajectory is as simple a condition to analyse as fifty; a hundred; a thousand men and several thousand projectiles is for me.

And speed is simply not an issue for time itself is but a factor in the equation. Time; space and motion. These three are as much my triumvirate my triumvirate (*sic*) as are Father, Son and Holy Ghost and, believe me, Doctor, I know this to be no blasphemy. For they, too are of Him, with Him and in Him. There is a form and purpose to existence, which, although it eludes me at the present time, hovers on the fringe of my vision. There is Order even in even in (*sic*) Chaos and all things are impelled. Duality is a mistaken concept. Things simply are the way they are. All things are no more than probability but there is isis (*sic*) a substance to it.

Doctor, forgive me. I am a little tired and I know that I have begun to ramble. Reading this, your face will have taken on an aspect that I might recognise as having seen regularly on my friend and comrade, Pte Lear! I no longer concern myself with re-drafting my letters to you, Doctor, for I know that you derive some interest from my idiosyncrasies.

Please would you be so good as to pass on my best wishes to Dr. Charteris. I have written a separate letter to her which is, I fancy, rather more coherent than this one, being as it is, written in the language of mathematics.

Yours sincerely

Cpl. Henry Lawrence.

ITEM: 23/03/17   Letter.   Sir Maxwell Cavendish to   Dr. James Pennyworth

Professor Sir Maxwell Cavendish
Royal Middlesex Hospital
London W12

23/03/1917
Dr. James Pennyworth
Royal Victoria Hospital,
Netley
Hants.

My Dear James,

Congratulations, my boy! The formal acceptance has been sent, of course but I simply couldn't resist dropping you this note.

Lady Frances and I could not be more delighted. On the occasion that we met Dr. Charteris and yourself at Claridge's just before Christmas, Lady Frances was, on the return journey, quite aquiver with the possibility that you might be rather more than colleagues. I told her not to be so foolish but, alas, once more she has proved to be the wiser of us!

We shall of course, be delighted to attend your wedding. Lady Frances has already alerted Mme. Chalons, her couturier and, no doubt, my tailor will be around in due course. Yet, I shall bear his ministrations with fortitude, James when I think of the cause for which they are borne!

Our best to you, dear fellow,

Sir Maxwell and Lady Cavendish.

Spring 1917

ITEM: 22/04/17 Letter. Pte George Lear to Mother (excerpt)

Ypres
22nd May 1917

Mrs Hilda Lear,
43 Kennet Terrace
Bradfield
West Riding of Yrks.

Dear Mother,

This afternoon, a most surprising thing happened.

We're sitting around in the dugout waiting to be sent
for, to return to the rear, when the blanket over the
door is swept back and in walks an officer - a major.

We all stand to attention and Captain Glendenning,
looking very surprised and caught without his cap,
snaps off a salute. The officer taps his own cap with
his stick and says, "At ease," as friendly as you
like. Then he walks straight over to my pal, Henry
Lawrence and embraces him like a long-lost brother!

'They tell me, Henry," (Henry!), he says, that you're
"popping" off to "Pop" this evening. Perhaps you'd
like to join me, as my guest, in a bite to eat! You
might like to bring one of your chums along.'
Lawrence looks at me and says he'd like that very
much. So, the next thing we know, were driving along
in an officer's staff car towards a slap-up meal! I
felt quite the toff, I can tell you.

I thought "popping" off to "Pop" was a very good
joke.

It turns out that this is Dr. James Pennyworth, the
medical man, who has taken something of a shine to
Lawrence, having been his Doctor these two years. He
was very civil to me, as well. He had come all this
way from England just to deliver a parcel. I expect
it was something mathematical, knowing Henry......

123

Maj. James Pennyworth

Talbot House

Poperinghe

Belgium

25/04/17

Dr Caroline Charteris

73 Hanover Square

Mayfair

London W

My Dear Caroline,

How I miss you! It seems an age since we parted at Victoria, although I know it was barely a week ago. I am staying, as you will see from the return address, at the famous Toc.H! I have a very comfortable room, which I share with a fellow by the name of Brand who seems a decent sort. And, because I am so far behind the lines and am leaving in a day or so, I feel I will not be distressing you as to my own condition if I recount to you the circumstances in which poor Lawrence and his comrades find themselves.

The mud and the filth cannot be imagined. Men in the trenches spend the entire day up to their knees in water. I know I said that I would try to steer clear of medical matters whilst I was here but one simply cannot ignore the plight of these chaps. I have seen case after case of trench-foot and bronchial infections of every kind and, although well fed, the infantry are in desperate want of dry clothing and shelter. I'll wager that for all who fall victim to the enemy, at least half as many again are laid low by illness and sheer exhaustion. I heard of a terrible incident in which a man fell asleep and simply drowned where he lay and, having seen where so many of them sleep, I can easily credit it.

And throughout all of this, the trenches are under constant attack from trench mortars and sniper fire. I asked Captain Glendenning if I might take a peek at the enemy through a loop hole, which is a tiny hole no more than an inch in diameter, in an armoured steel plate. He strongly advised against it, saying that Fritz would notice the movement at once and would be able to send a rifle bullet straight through it without it touching the side! I could see by his face that he was in earnest.

I then asked if I might use a periscope. Again, he warned that it might be a deadly mistake for me to do so. I wondered if he might be being a little over-cautious but not a bit of it. It is possible, apparently for a German sniper on ground only a foot or so higher to spot the periscope rising up above the trench and for him to place his shot at a point just before the lip of the trench. The ground is so soft and the round so powerful, that it may pass directly through the mud and need only hit a loosely-packed or damaged sandbag, to emerge through the very wall of the trench and hit whomever is holding the periscope! Of course, our own snipers are playing the same game, so everyone scuttles about in a permanent crouch.

I asked Lawrence if he planned to use the range-finder to assist his own marksmanship. "With respect, Doctor," says he, "I can manage very well without it!" Impudence! But one forgives him, of course. It is just his way. He tells me, however, that he has plans to use it in what he terms a "more humane manner". What on earth could be "humane" about anything here is beyond me, I'm sure.

He thanks you for your "workings" as he calls them. In an effort to ensure he appreciates the amount of time you expend upon them, I made some comment to the effect and he acknowledged your labour with such deference, gratitude and respect that you would have blushed to hear him.

126

Ypres May 08 1917

I am becoming concerned for Lawrence. He has always been a brave fellow and a great one for inspiring confidence but lately, he seems to have become quite reckless. This afternoon, Captain Glendenning came along and asked for volunteers to carry a trench mortar and several boxes of ammunition to a beleaguered unit at Hooge. I immediately looked at the ground, only to hear Lawrence say,
"Lear and I will do it, Sir". When the Captain had gone, I said to Lawrence, quite smartly although he is corporal of our unit,
"That's the Menin Road, Lawrence! We'll be killed." He didn't seem to realise how angry and scared I was, for he said only,
"I should like to try something."

We waited until the sun was low in the sky (the Germans are at a disadvantage with the setting sun in their eyes.) The Captain gave me a map, (such as it was), said, "Keep to the ditches and you should be fine. Good luck", and off we went, Lawrence carrying the heavy trench mortar across his back and a box of rifle ammunition in his hand. I carried another ammunition box upon my back and we carried the extremely heavy mortar shells in a box hanging between us as we scurried along. Of course, we also had our own kit and rifles and, in addition, Lawrence carried a collapsible tripod that he insisted on bringing.

Every agonising step, I was certain would be our last but Lawrence was cheerful, as always. I was still quite angry with him and I told him so.
"Come, George", he said, "let me tell you why I am not concerned."
"I'm all ears," I said to him, rather coldly.
"I am going to destroy an enemy gun." Lawrence said.

Presently, we reached the sunken road, which the Germans know is a place where men, against all advice feel safe, it being high walled, like a trench, on both sides. Naturally, Fritz has it permanently in his sights and so wise men do not stop there for long in case Fritz decides to chance a pot-shot. Countless otherwise sensible fellows have come badly unstuck at this place and I did not wish to join their number. As we entered this dangerous region, Lawrence signalled for us to rest and my heart sank. The road and its embankments are pitted with shell holes and Lawrence guided me over towards one of these. Of course, it was full of water, but Lawrence went in up to his thighs.

"Do you see this ridge?" he asked, pointing to a raised area on the edge of the hole. "Well, this is the end farthest from the blast. The earth was flung in this direction," he pointed, "which means the shell was fired from the opposite direction."
"And this is your marvellous system?" I asked. "I know where the Germans are!" His smile never faltered.
"Do you see all the pits surrounding the hole and the lumps of mud, which have been flung out from the explosion?"
"I have been intimately familiar with such this twelvemonth." I said.

At this point, however, I began to understand what Lawrence was getting at. "Wait a moment," I said, "do you mean to tell me that your mathematics can deduce from the pattern beneath us, ruined as it is by further shelling and by the elements, the exact position of the gun that made it?"
"Provided the gun is still there, as I suspect it is, yes. Yes, it can." He stepped out of the hole and made a beeline for the embankment. He flattened himself against it and, a moment later, I lay alongside. Lawrence fished in his tunic and removed an instrument, which I had never before seen.

I asked him what it was and he told me that it was a range-finder of his own design, which Dr. Pennyworth had arranged to have made for him in Southampton. "Where did you get the money to pay for it?" I asked in astonishment. Apparently, the doctor had had it made at his own expense! It required a little assembly and when, at last, he was finished, Lawrence set it on the tripod he'd brought and put his eye to it. Moments later, having unpacked the mortar, he was on his hands and knees beside it. After only a few seconds, he grabbed the shell I was holding (under his orders) and the mortar was fired. I could not see how it could avoid attracting attention, but Lawrence was unconcerned. The mortar landed a thousand yards away with a huge crash, sending debris high into the air. I clearly saw the barrel of a German gun and a wheel fly up. Lawrence had got it with the first shot! I know he is a fine marksman but a trench mortar is not a rifle. Far from it, in fact. I was still staring, open mouthed as the machine guns opened up on our position but, with Lawrence leading the way, we were soon back in the ditch on the far side of the road, lost to sight. That didn't stop the enemy sending the odd burst over the road but we eventually arrived safely. The officer in charge said we were a welcome crew and he found us a dry billet for the night.

Lawrence said I was not to mention anything of what he had done on the Menin Road that night and nor did I. I wish I knew what went on his mind.

Summer 1917

ITEM: 09/08/17 Letter. The Hon. Charles Hardwicke to Dr. Caroline Charteris

Sqdn. Cmdr. Charles Hardwicke
1st Wing Royal Flying Corps
Flanders
9th August 1917

Dr. Caroline Charteris
24 Hanover Square
Mayfair
London

Darling Carrie,

Well, old thing, it looks like they're going to let me back to Blighty for your big day! Just as well, too. Getting a bit peppery over here at the moment.

After Messines, everyone thought it was pretty much all done and dusted. Mines destroy enemy front line, Fritz on the run and all that. (Hell of a bang, Carrie! They say it was heard in London but, I suppose you'd have had to have been listening, eh?) Anyway, brass has torn it again. They've been battering Fritz's fall-back trenches for about a fortnight, now but it looks like the Somme all over again.

The Germans are dug in so deep, our shells have about as much effect on them as a spring shower on a lettuce. My lads have told 'em the wire's still intact but no-one's taking any notice. And you would not credit the rain! It's been chucking it down solidly for a week and most of our shells just go "plop" rather than "bang"! I can't imagine how much unexploded ordnance there is in these fields. I wouldn't recommend driving a plough into the ground anywhere round here for a long while.

131

This place is such a bally mess, we can scarce get a kite off the ground. Spend practically all day filling in craters. Persuaded a young oik to take me up for a shufti yesterday and I'll swear I saw nothing even remotely green within forty miles of Ypres. Can't tell you how much I'm looking forward to seeing the English countryside again. Funny, really. Couldn't wait to get back here and now I can't wait to leave. It might be different if they'd let me fly.

I can't help wondering if they've agreed to my leave because they want shot of me! Can't blame 'em. Making a bit of a nuisance of myself, actually. But can you believe they still won't let me take a kite up!? What's the point of being a Squadron Commander if they won't let you fly a bally aeroplane? I took the Bristol out practically every day during convalescence. The old peg-leg works a treat with only a little modification and Brandywine has already bodged up one of the new Sopwiths so I'm ready to go. There's nothing in regs to say a one-legged pilot can't go up! You feel so useless stuck on the ground, Carrie. I don't know how the infantry bods do it, frankly.

Anyway, mustn't get maudlin, eh? Felicitations to all who give a tinker's, Carrie and see you at St. Barnabas' on the 18th! Bags the first dance!

Pip pip

Charlie

132

19th August 1917

Mrs. James Pennyworth
73 Hanover Square
Mayfair
London W

Dear Dr. Pennyworth,

It seems most strange to be addressing my own doctor and yet writing to his wife! You may even think it impertinent but your husband wrote informing me of your happy event and I make no apology. I rejoice at the news!

These new equations are the result of deliberations following on from the earlier conjectures I have been sending these past months. They may be worthless beyond their value as a model but they are by far, the most beautiful and elegant thing within several hundred miles of this dreadful place and, since I know for certain that without the kindness of you and your husband, it would have been far beyond my power to communicate to you, I offer them as an insight to my world. My wish, I suppose, is that they might bring you here, as well - metaphorically, of course! They are my gift to you.

Firstly, this *(sic)* you will remember this: (The first option is from Riemann, the second is my own)

$$\zeta(s) = \sum_{-}(n = 1) \; 1/n \wedge s \quad \text{OR} \quad \prod_{-}p \, (1 - 1 \, /p \wedge s) \wedge (-1)$$

And, bearing in mind the data, which I have already supplied:

$$\mu B = (\varepsilon\eta)/(2m\_c) = ((c\_(0) \,_{00} \wedge 5 \, h) \, / \, (32\pi_\wedge(2) \, (\mu\_OR)_\wedge(2)\,_{00}))$$

And

$C\_(Nexp) \; (-N/(2) \; tr \; (H \wedge 2) \,) \; where \; C\_(N)$
$(2\pi) - (N(N+1))/2 \; N_\wedge(N \wedge 2)/2$

You will recognise Planck's Constant but as for the rest, you should find that it follows on from some of the earlier proofs I sent. Note the Gaussian nature of the second formula.

I shall not be offended if you see fit to correct any of these equations. I know on the face of it, they appear quite insane but, since they describe something of how I perceive the world, that should not be so surprising, should it?

Cpl. Henry Lawrence.

Autumn 1917

ITEM: 21/09/17 Letter. George Lear to Parents

Ypres,
Belgium
21st September 1917

Mr and Mrs John Lear,
43 Kennet Terrace
Bradfield
West Riding of Yrks.

Dear Mother and Father,

Well, it's a damp old day, as usual! The rain hasn't stopped for weeks now and the whole of Flanders appears to be just one giant lake. Our lads are all soaked through for days at a stretch. Luckily, I have been able to secure a nice little billet in the dry thanks to my pal, Henry Lawrence who is valued so much by our officers that they try to look after him that little bit better. His marksmanship and his way with a mortar has saved our bacon a number of times, I can tell you.

Our only consolation as far as the rain is concerned is that it falleth on both the just and the unjust! Fritz is no doubt as wet as we are.

I got your cake and very welcome it was. My second birthday in the trenches; who would have thought it? I hope my next one will be at home. I do miss you all but I have more work to do here and I'm determined to see it through. Keep your chins up.

Your son,

George Lear

Ypres September 21 1917

This is the twentieth day of rain. Trench collapse this morning saw fifteen lads drowned in the mud. As we were digging them out, we came upon bodies from goodness knows how many battles past. When you fall, dead or alive, the mud takes you and you sort of swim around in it for days. It has no more solidity than pea soup. Where and when you turn up again is anyone's guess. Since Cartwright drowned, I can't get his face out of my head. Until the day I die, I shall see him, arms outstretched, begging me to save him. And then, at the last, as the mud filled his mouth, begging me to kill him. Had Lawrence not done the deed, I think my nightmares would have been unbearable.

Lawrence has wangled a cushy little number guarding the ammunition. It's the only dry spot in this section and he is able to sneak me in occasionally. Never long enough to dry out completely but enough to take the chill away for an hour or two. He is good sort and I am happy that our officers are beginning to see his worth. Compared to many folk out here, he now seems quite sane!

He said to me,
'George, this War is coming to an end. I believe we're in for a rough few months first, though. There is a German offensive in the offing.'

'How can you be sure?' I asked, rather foolishly, since he would never be able to explain. He just smiled his smile.

I know that it is his mathematics that tells him these things, otherwise I might be rather afraid of him – as anyone would be – for soldiers are a superstitious lot. He knows this and so I think I'm the only one he confides in.

But I sometimes wonder. If he can work these things out, why can't the top brass? They must have far more information than he does. He reads the Gazette and he listens to the officers and says he can see patterns that are always changing and, at some point, they resolve and point in only one direction. How numbers can do all that is beyond me. Anyway, if he thinks we'll soon be going home, that is as cheery a thought as I have had in months.

He did say one chilling thing, though, about the German communication lines. Railways and the like. They've always had excellent methods of getting their supplies forward and whenever they break through, their supplies follow on quite quickly. Our lines stop at Pop and then it all has to be dragged through the mud by hand. Lawrence is going to try to persuade Capt. Glendenning to warn our brass about the German supply lines. If they can be broken, Lawrence says, any offensive is bound to fail. I don't see how we can possibly break their lines. We can't even move men in this mud, let alone guns.

I told Lawrence this and he says to me (and I got him to say it again slowly, so I could write it down),

"There is a tide in the affairs of men.
Which, taken at the flood, leads on to fortune;
Omitted, all the voyage of their life
Is bound in shallows and in miseries.
On such a full sea are we now afloat,
And we must take the current when it serves,
Or lose our ventures."

I swear, he grows odder.

(I have learnt from one of the lads that this is from William Shakespeare. He can't remember the play. If this is what Shakespeare is like, I want to read more.)

ITEM: 16/10/17 Letter. Dr. James Pennyworth to Private George Lear

Dr. James Pennyworth

Royal Victoria Hospital,

Netley

Hants.

16/10/17

Dear Private Lear,

My dear fellow, please do not trouble yourself over protocol. Our evening at De Oude Kerk established your right to address me directly.

I can fully understand your concern over Lawrence but as his doctor, and since, (by your own account) he knows nothing of our correspondence, I am not at liberty to discuss any matter with you concerning his condition.

However, the matter of which you write is, I might say, intriguing.

Your Captain is worthy of much admiration for taking it upon himself to speak on our friend's behalf although I'm not surprised that he has been unsuccessful and Lawrence's own efforts were certainly doomed to failure. It is remarkable to learn of any man approaching his superiors with plans of action, but the fact that he has escaped charge thus far is little short of a wonder. He is doubtless of more worth in the lines than tied to a gun wheel.

Lawrence has surprised a good few people in the course of this war and it would not surprise _me_ were he to do so again but you should advise him, as will I, that not everyone respects his insights to the same extent that you and I have come to do. Should you doubt this, then only think back to the first time you encountered him and the effect his demeanour and his statements had upon you. I can be certain of your conclusions, for although my early dealings with him left me bewildered, I had no sense whatsoever of being in the presence of genius.

My wife it was who revealed to me the potential of a mind such as Henry's, to perceive so fully the workings of the world. He is no Mr. Dick dancing to a different drummer; he is a savant of the highest order. I should trust his insights with my very life but fear, at this rate, they may well be the death of him.

Once again, Lear, I implore you to impress upon him the importance of discretion in the matter of his skill.

I shall, of course, not mention in my own letter that you have been in touch.

Until I have the pleasure of your company, once more, I remain

Yours truly,

Dr. J. Pennyworth.

Spring 1918

ITEM: 30/03/18 Letter. Maj. Dr. Pennyworth to Pte. Lawrence

Dear Henry,

It shames me to admit that I had so little faith in your abilities. As I now learn, the information you sent me regarding the German counter offensive was correct to almost every degree but you must realise how difficult it would have been for me to have even broached the subject with anyone capable of acting upon it. As I explained in my last letter, I am a doctor. My military rank is a courtesy, no more. I would not have been believed. It may be of some consolation to you, however, that my dear wife championed your cause against me until the last although even she could not fully understand what you were proposing we should do.

May I reiterate what I have already told you; however convinced you may be, you must never again speak of these things to anyone. I tremble to think what could happen were it to be thought that you possessed intelligence rightfully known only by the Germans themselves.

Through God's Grace and good fortune, we shall halt the enemy advance and regain our lost ground. We must. For it must never be countenanced that so many men may have died in vain. That we have lost all the ground and more that was so hard won in the previous three years is a terrible thing and we must not falter in our resolve.

Please take care, Henry and, once more, forgive me for doubting you.

Dr. James Pennyworth.

ITEM 05/04/18 Letter, Cpl Lawrence to Dr. James Pennyworth

Ypres

5 April 1918

Maj. Dr. Pennyworth
Royal Victoria Hospital,
Netley
Hants.

Dear Doctor,

There is nothing at all to forgive. I have been considering my actions and I realise that I must have placed you in an invidious position. It was foolish of me to imagine that any of our commanders would pay any more attention to you than they would to me, even were I to gain any sort of access.

Indeed, on the face of it, my proposal seems to lack any shred of common sense, a fact, which (whilst I have for some time realised that common sense has nothing to do with how the world seems to function) I realise is dreadfully difficult for most people to ignore. It was many months before I was able to abandon it myself.

"Common sense": A curious term, don't you think, Doctor? For were even the most basic understanding of the motives, minds and hearts of men commonly sensed, might we not have avoided the awful circumstances in which now find ourselves? Yet, that we had to stop the Germans, I'm afraid I have no doubt. As the entirety of the conflict becomes visible to me, so I become certain that, but for our heeding the call of our allies, the Germans would have swept across Europe and, believe me, things would have been even worse than they are at present – difficult as that may be to understand.

But I do not believe the Germans to be evil nor particularly wicked – nor, of course do they, themselves (the inscription on their belt buckles is "Gott mit uns", after all) and I do not doubt

that they believe it. It is simply that they, like
us, follow orders.

And our Chaplain assures us that God is with the
Allies, too. How may that be, Doctor? All I can
imagine is that God is as torn as any parent who
sees his children argue and even come to blows. He
will not – cannot – take sides, one over the other
but can only do all in his power to ensure that
neither is so badly damaged that reconciliation is
not possible. But, Doctor, if I can see what must
be done, why can God Himself not see; and act?

Am I tempting my God by wondering this? I can only
pray that His purpose is so far above the
pettynesses of our world that it is one of those
several things that is simply not visible to me.
And I ask you, in all seriousness, do you believe
it Blasphemy for me to believe that my current
circumstance puts me in a position to act as an
instrument of the Lord?

Killing has never been an easy matter for me – nor,
I'm happy to report, for most of my comrades – but
now that I see more - and that more clearly - it is
far, far worse. For I know that the greater part
of those I kill are dying in vain; not only, you
understand, from the point of view of their friends
and their families but also from my own. For I can
see that their deaths and those of my own comrades
serve our cause not one jot and thus, the killing
is, (and this is no glib use of the term), futile.

It must cease. It must cease.

Summer 1918

ITEM: 18/07/18 Communiqué. Lt. Col. Horace Barham to Maj.
Spencer Wills

```
                             Lt. Col. Horace Barham
        Officer Commanding 4ᵗʰ Wing Royal Air Force,
                                           Boesinghe
                                            Flanders
                                       July 18th 1918
```

Major Spencer Wills
Acting Sqdn. Cmdr.
23ʳᵈ Sqdn
Zonnevelt Airfield

Major Wills,
I know it's a bloody thing but this Hardwicke business
is getting ridiculous. The fellow must have a string of
connections a mile long, for I have been fairly
bombarded with petitions on his behalf. I have tapped
most of them to mid-wicket, in spite of the odd googly,
but it's all getting a bit tiresome.

Fact is the new Brigadier General has also made it
abundantly clear that he wants nothing to do with
sending cripples to fight. He feels it would not go
down well with the public. I have tried to persuade him
to the contrary, pointing out that the Air Ministry has
established the valiant Fighter Ace as something of a
totem nowadays and to see Hardwicke and the others
hopping over the field for a crack at the enemy would
swell the heart; strengthen the old sinews, and what
have you.

However, he does not see it my way; reckons the Royal
Air Force is a more professional outfit than the old
R.F.C. and so again I must ask that you pass on the
decision of Command that flying is out of the question
but reassure Hardwicke that his rank remains unaltered
and that, as Recording Officer, he is performing a
valuable service and all that.

And tell him to lay off the sauce a bit, will you. Word
has got back and it won't do.

Barham

147

ITEM: 01/08/18 Letter. The Hon. Charles Hardwicke to Dr. Caroline Pennyworth

```
                           Sqdn. Cmdr. Charles Hardwicke
                           23rd Sqdn. Royal Flying Corps
                                                 Flanders
                                         1st August 1918
```

Dr. Caroline Pennyworth
66 Hanover Square
Mayfair
London

Dear Carrie,

Well, they've turned me down again, old thing and I really think this is it. They have no intention of ever letting me fly and we're losing scores of pilots each day! Some of them have just three hours under their belt. It's no wonder they don't last above a week, most of 'em. I have over 1400 hours and 26 kills, Carrie and they won't let me fly! But I have an idea.

You remember, many moons since, you asked me to keep an eye out for that corporal - maths bod who's been writing to you – patient of James's? Well, he was pointed out to me a week or two back at Toc H. We fell a-nattering and he told me a few things. I was feeling a bit in the dumps at the time, of course but talking to him really perked me up. Don't know why. The odd thing was - he said he'd been looking out for me, too.

I know you told him I was in the same general area but do you know what the chances of us both running into one another like that must be? Kismet, old Carrie, is what I call it!

Anyway, the fellow comes up with this rum idea about him and me going off to find a few railway lines to knock out. Well, of course I thought he was pulling my leg (ha ha) but not a bit of it. He had drawings and maps and all sorts of gubbins.

'Course, then I reckoned he was off his rocker but as he spoke it became clear that he might just have something.

148

I didn't bother to ask why he hadn't gone to the brass with it. I went to school with half of them and a less imaginative bunch you wouldn't care to meet. I asked if he knew what would happen to us if we tried it and, do you know what he said? "It's not important"! "It might not be important to you, old fruit," was my rejoinder, "but it's ruddy life and death to me."

I told him that even if I could get the chance, (thinking the while about Brandywine's work on my kite), did he have any idea how difficult it is to drop a bomb on a railway line from fifteen hundred feet? And he wouldn't get anyone to fly much below that in daylight for starters! Look at poor old McCudden; seventy four kills and he's knocked on the head by some Hun with a pop gun at tree top height!

But Lawrence reckons that with his little book and a stub of pencil and that little gadget your hubby made for him (which, he tells me has taught him all he needs to know about gyroscopic bomb sighting), he could drop a bomb on a pickelhaub if he had to! And I can't think why, but I believe him.

Well, this is the real point of this missive, old thing. You see, I've decided to go along with his loony scheme. The way I see it, I've nothing to lose. It'll give me one last go at the Germans and what's the RFC or "Royal Air Force" as they're styling themselves now, going to do? Ground me? (Ho! Ho!). I've no intention of making this a suicide mission, though, so don't go all weak at the knees just yet. I want to see the look on old Horace's face when I get back.

I'm the last of them, you know. Jimmy, Corny, Willans, Rats: all gone, now. And here I am a blasted Recording Officer, tied to a desk. Whoops! Self-pity. Won't do! But it is a bit daring and all that, so, should the worst happen, think of me fondly, dear old Carrie, as I think of you. Give my best to your old man too, while you're at it.

Pip pip!

Charlie.

I had never seen my friend so agitated. He always loved Talbot House and was usually at his most relaxed there. For several hours, he had been writing in a little notebook. It was utter gobbledygook, of course, equations and such and I knew there was no point asking him about it. Then, quite suddenly, his mood changed entirely and the smile that had played upon his lips practically the whole time I had known him, returned. It had been absent for a number of days. He told me that he would not be returning to the billet that night and that this would be the last time he and I would speak.

I told him not to be such a fool but there was one thing you could count upon; when he said something, there was usually no contradicting it. He stood up and buttoned his tunic.

'You will be a fine poet, one day, George; I have no doubt,' he said and moved towards the door. I said something along the lines of him outdoing himself in oddness, this evening but he made no reply.

I made to speak again but he turned and gave me so smart and so final a salute that I could not utter a word. I neither saw nor heard of him again.

For some reason, there was no muster the following day and two skirmishes had left a number of our lads missing. I wrote his name down as being one of those. I knew it was wrong, of course but I did it, nevertheless. I would not have wanted him to be thought a coward and a deserter. For, though he may have been the latter, he most certainly was not the former.

ITEM: 08/08/18   Communiqué.   Lt. Col. Horace Barham to Maj. Spencer Wills

```
                        Lt. Col. Horace Barham
        Officer Commanding 4ᵗʰ Wing Royal Air Force,
                                       Boesinghe
                                       Flanders
                                August 8th 1918
```

```
Major Spencer Wills
Acting Sqdn. Cmdr.
23ʳᵈ Sqdn
Zonnevelt Airfield
```

Major,

Am I to take it that <u>no-one</u> now has any idea of the whereabouts of the aeroplane that took off this morning from your airstrip? How in blazes can this happen? Had you not realised that Squadron Commander Hardwicke had intimated that he might do just this sort of thing, once his request to be allowed airborne had been finally refused? Why was he not kept away from the machines?

There are reports of him landing on the airstrip at Poperinghe and taking on board several cans of fuel, ammunition and a passenger. He was last seen heading towards German lines. If that passenger turns out to be a spy, I cannot hold out any hope of you avoiding a Court-Martial.

If Hardwicke has not returned by 19:30 hours, I want him posted "Missing In Action" NOT "Absent Without Leave". Airmen are not cowards. I hope I make myself clear. As soon as you have done this, I shall want to see you over here to answer in person for your conduct.

Barham

ITEM: 08/08/18   A Black Day– *The End of Germany's War in Europe*
***1918* (excerpts)   Heinrich Bakker 2010**

Even as early as August 12th 1918, General Ludendorff was making references to *"Der schwarze Tag der deutschen Armee"* The famous "Black Day". It was clear even then that the French and American divisions had won a famous victory and the war was all but lost.

Ludendorff had clearly over-stretched himself. Even with the recall of men and materiel from the Eastern Front, there were simply not enough troops to out-manoeuvre the combined might of France and the U.S. But it was not merely the losses in France, on the Marne and the Aisne, which defeated the Germans, vital though these were. For the supply lines were far from secure at this stage in the War and the German soldiers were hungry and short of materiel.

They were particularly enraged to find that, despite the propaganda, which had told them British supply lines had been compromised by U-boat action, the British trenches they captured appeared well-stocked with fresh as well as tinned food..."[3]

...The part played by the failure of German supply lines cannot be overstated. According to Professor Heinz Leimann of The University of Bonn;

> *".....if there was a true turning point in the War, it*
> *would be the loss of the Lille to Brussels rail link in*
> *the north and the Laon – Charleroi in the south,*
> *which combined, left over 800,000 troops and*
> *supplies stranded in the middle of Belgium, too far*
> *away to assist their comrades in the west and too*
> *distant from Berlin to survive alone for long....."* [6]

Epilogue Spring 1933

ITEM: 04/05/33   Extract from the private papers of Dr. Caroline Pennyworth.

Mayerhofen, Austria, 1933

Dark days are coming. One does not need to be a professional mathematician to realise that. And barely fifteen years after the end of the Great War. It hardly seems possible here, surrounded by the magnificence of these mountains so steadfast, unheeding and untouched by the petty squabbles of men. They have always been and will always be. Yet, no, of course they will not. We fleeting little animals simply move too quickly to perceive their vast, majestic dance; yet dance they surely do. And do they, these monuments to the birth-pangs of our world; do they in turn, I wonder perceive God in the manner we perceive them? If so, then what must we be to God? Mere flyspecks, lasting a bare instant of time to His eyes. That cannot be. For did he not set us in motion? Time and space are nought to Him.

Time, Space and Motion. How prophetic Lawrence's words have proven to be! What that man must have known. He tried to tell me but it was so far beyond my powers to appreciate. Even now, after all these years, his equations obscure more than they reveal. He appears to have had an answer before there was even a question to be asked!

Missing. That's all it said. Lawrence, Charlie and the rest. Nourishing the land around Ypres, engaged in an eternal dance of their own, these…boys. Names on an archway; memories, only.

154

And now my own dear James is but a memory, also. I thank God for the years we had, for our children and for the life we made. His strength and his courage are with me still, as I mourn his loss. I do not cry. I make plans. Now that Dr. Schrodinger has decided to leave for England and has asked for me to accompany him, I believe it will herald a new chapter in my life. If he takes up the position at Oxford, then I shall be working alongside old friends and colleagues. I am convinced that my best work is ahead of me. Who knows; perhaps one day, I might even understand what Lawrence was trying to teach me.

I almost hear Charlie's voice as I write..."Chin up, old thing! Mustn't dwell and all that."

End

Addendum
Poems of George Lear *(1898-1980)* that reference Henry Lawrence

The Stone (1916)

One summer's morn, the sergeant asked,
politely, as always;
If we would mind a-falling in,
(He's a lovely turn of phrase).
And so we rose, put on our kit
And waited for the call
And it's "Move out chaps,
If you'd be so kind."
And we answered, "Not at all!"

But I hadn't gone but seven steps
Before I pulled up short.
The chap behind, crashed into me
I'm sorry to report.
An officer rode over then;
I snapped off a salute.
And since he asked, I told him:
"I've got a stone inside me boot!"

"A stone inside your boot?" he says,
"One stone; I'll tell you straight,
There's eighteen stone inside that boot;
You need to lose some weight".
He laughed and I felt foolish
Just like a raw recruit
I'd been gone and made a fool of by
The stone inside me boot!

They wouldn't stop nor even slow
The pace to give me ease,
We had to march up to the front
To fight our enemies.
 I would have faced a thousand foes,
No matter their repute
If it would mean I could remove
The stone inside me boot!

So I shook the stone down to the front
And wrapped me toe around
And there, I swear, it nestled
Until suddenly I found,
It had an even sharper bit
A blade edge so acute
It would have made the parson swear;
The stone inside me boot!

Then Henry turns and says to me,
Don't worry about the stone,
Imagine it the seed from which
The Tree of Life was grown.
When I looked (you won't believe)
Blow me, there was a root
A growin' from the lace holes
From the stone inside me boot!

Now what you do, old Henry says,
Is imagine that the tree
Grows feather pillows, thistledown
And woollen finery
And that your foot is bound with fur
The pain for to dilute.
No more will you be troubled by
The stone inside your boot!

So all day long, mile after mile,
I thought that pain away
I never would have thought it true
Nor would you I daresay
And when we reached the forward trench
I said "Thank you, old fruit"
To my pal who helped me think away
The stone inside me boot!

And if ever you should feel the sting
Of stone or twig or thorn,
Remember that discomfort may
With fortitude be borne.
For the British Soldier and his wits
Full sharpened and acute
Come what may, can walk all day
With a stone inside his boot!

The Dream (1918)

Last night, as soldiers will, too deeply of red wine I drank
And slept beneath the sky
And, as I slumbered there, I dreamed of those companions lost
Or driven out to die in muddy fields, forgotten holes
Yet never knowing why.

And one, my dearest friend, stood by me even as I woke,
(Though I knew it could not be)
Since now I slept no more, and yet he smiled and spoke:
Of wonders he could see; then (as he could not in life),
He showed his world to me.

And here, awake I seem, although I fancy still I dream but
Nature proves me wrong
For, upon my aching head, cool dew I feel, scent honeyed
meadow-sweet,
Taste bitterness on wine-dry tongue. And see aloft, the careless
lark.
She circles still, the clouds among;

She circles yet, upon her song.
She circles yet;
Upon her song.

Remembering Things To Come
– written at the Armistice 1918

And we will remember
Where we were; what we were doing
When we learned hostilities would cease
At the eleventh hour and the eleventh month.
And we'll remember the face
Of him who gave the news,
Our reluctance to believe and our bewildered joy.

And we will remember
Who was there and what they said
As the silence bloomed like a summer rose
And fell o'er the dark, grey and wintry field.
And we'll remember how it grew
In the trenches and the dugouts;
Our reluctance to hear and our unshed tears.

And we will remember
How it felt as the train drew nigh
And we clambered aboard for that journey home
And that interminable voyage: one day, one night, no more
And we'll remember how it felt
To tread upon our isle at last
To see our loved ones there,
Our hesitance to embrace and our timid smiles.

And we will remember
Once all these trials are past
The friends who fell; that cruel lie!
They did not fall: they were cut down and torn
To pieces 'fore our eyes and spread upon the land.
And we'll remember how it was
At Passchendaele and Broodesinde.
Our need to laugh away our agonised torment.

And I will remember
What he said and how he smiled
Though neither shall I ever truly understand
But know that I saw God in both those things.
For he remembered things to come:
And I cannot forget my sorrow
At his inability to explain and mine to understand.

Also By Russell Cruse

It was never going to be easy taking twenty teenagers skiing in the Alps but it wasn't half so difficult as returning with only nineteen.

When fifteen- year-old Carly Elliot parts company with an Alp, David Benedict, the teacher in charge of the ski-party is suspended from his job pending charges of negligence and possibly even manslaughter.

His only ally is journalist Rebecca Daley and even she's trying to connect him to two teenage suicides.

Polizeikommissar Kurz thinks David may be a murderer, D.S. Sands thinks he's an idiot and the others down the nick reckon he's a paedophile but it won't be until he finds himself tied to a chair in a run-down church, an automatic pistol in his face and trying desperately, through broken teeth, to speak German with a Swiss accent that he'll begin to suspect he may be in over his head.

Could things get any worse? Of course they can; this is David Benedict we're talking about.

Daley wants a story, Benedict wants his old life back; if either gets what they want, the other will be seriously disappointed. In the event, each of them is going to get a bloody sight more than they bargained for.

'Ah well; another day, another death. Welcome to St. Wilf's.'

Available through AMAZON as a paperback or on Kindle.

Author website: www.russellcruse.com

162